Warrior King Saint

Sebastian Swan

Book 2 in the "Ulfberht" series

Prologue

This story is the sequel to "The Price of Honour".

The Price of Honour was the tale of a young warrior, commissioned to bring a beautiful young girl to Bernicia. (Modern day Northumbria)

The girl had been chosen to be the wife of the great King Æthelfrith.

Tragically, the young warrior and the princess are touched by the gods and love was the price of that brush with another world.

In the end, the lover's died for their innocence, *but* a child is born from their love and he is called

"Oswald".

Oswald

Dedicated to my wife for all the years of love.

"Love has nothing to do with what you are
expecting to get – only with what you are
expecting to give – which is everything."
– Katharine Hepburn –

Thanks to:

Carolyn: for all her enduring support and kindness, she is truly an extraordinary person.
Pat: for all her hard work and years of friendship.

This book is a work of fiction and should not be understood in any other sense. It is set in the context of history to give the story literary credibility. Many of the place names in this book are real, but their descriptions do not necessarily portray accurately the places mentioned. Most of the characters are historically authentic. All thoughts or comments, speech and opinions are from the author's own imagination and should not be attributed to any third party, unless otherwise stated. Historical information has on occasion been adjusted to fit the story

The cover artwork is by the author.

If the reader has any comments about the book, the author would be pleased to hear from you.

sebastian.dave.swan@gmail.com

Sebastian Swan was born in the North East of England not far from Bamburgh, he lectured in Yorkshire then, as the salmon returns to the place of its birth, he returned to the North East when he retired and began writing. All his life he had struggled with the written word, being dyslexic. Where he did excel, was his artwork, he drew and painted from being a small boy.

He had cancer, which forced him to retire, while he was ill he started to read for pleasure, he couldn't do much else for a while. He found that in reading he could be transported away from the pain to another place, a "Dream World".

One day he thought he could create his own dream world, he would do it through writing, with a little help from his friends, and draw from the vast resources of history and beauty on his doorstep. Writing, he thought, was only an extension of his childhood games. The only limitations were down to imagination.

Most of his books are played out in the beautiful North East of England, where the places in the books can be seen and touched.

Come to the North East, sit on the quiet beaches, close your eyes, and be transported into the world of Sebastian Swan.

David Mattches BA

Follow Sebastian Swan on "Face Book".

Chapters

Chapter 1

Escape

Pungent, dirty brown and white foam blew from the withers of the exhausted ponies as they thundered west. Their nostrils flared as they galloped, desperate to fill their burning lungs and bring relief to their aching muscles.

'*Cedric*,' a young boy called to his friend as he drew near to him. 'We will have to

1

rest soon, if not for Mother's sake, then for these poor animals.'

'I know Lord, I know...' Cedric conceded on hearing his own thoughts given flesh. '*Hrodulf,*' he in turn shouted to the rider before him. The warrior turned without breaking pace. 'We will stop at that thicket yonder.'

'I see it...' Hrodulf shouted back over his shoulder, at the same time adjusting the direction of his mount towards the wooded rise of silver birch. The rest followed, their horses stumbled and staggered the last few elnes [1] to the edge of the tree line and stopped. Cedric slid despondently from his hot saddle, which creaked and groaned in sympathy. He paused, straightened and stretched, pressing his hands into the small of his aching back, rubbed his leg and then went to the side of Queen Acha.

'My Lady,' he said bowing and offering his hand to her.

'Is it *safe* to stop here, Cedric?' she asked hesitantly, and glanced at Queen Bebba, without responding to the proffered hand.

Cedric thought how tired she looked, and not just from the unrelenting pace of the journey. The last years had been thorny for her. 'We have little choice, I fear, my Lady; our ponies can go no further unless they are rested. I can't see any pursuers and we have a clear view from this place. I'm confident that we are safe for the time being. We will only stay here until we, and our mounts, have had time to be refreshed and regain some strength. They are wiry little animals they will soon recover. Fear not my Lady, we'll make it to Ad Gefrin [2] and safety before nightfall.'

'If you say so Cedric, we will be guided by you,' she replied and only now leant forward so that the old warrior could take her by the waist and help her from her saddle. Though she was well able to ride, the pace had been frantic as they fled from her brother Edwin's forces heading north towards her home of Din Guyaroi, [3] or *Bebbanburg* [4] as some now called it, since Æthelfrith had taken his new wife Queen Bebba. Cedric and Queen Bebba were respectful to each other, but no more. He thought she was haughty and a schemer, ever trying to assert her will over Queen Acha who was gentle, like her sister Aefre, whom Cedric had loved.

His plan was to stay a night or so at Ad Gefrin, rest, take stock, and make sound preparation for the long journey ahead. He was sure King Edwin wouldn't waste his time following them as soon as his forces reached Din Guyaroi. Cedric's home would forever be Din Guyaroi to him, never Bebbanburg. The plan was then to head west to the Court of the Dalriadan [21] King, Eochaid Buide, the relative of Queen Bebba, and hope that he'd look favourably on them *all*.

Æthelfrith had spent many years suppressing the northern kingdoms; King Eochaid's amongst them, and now Æthelfrith's family would be seeking refuge with him. Cedric knew what he would do if he were Eochaid and who could blame him. Queen Bebba insisted that this was their only option and Cedric had reluctantly agreed, even though he knew that it would be difficult for Queen Acha. He would see that no harm came to her and he had made that known to Queen Bebba in no uncertain terms. He was a warrior who had earned his right to be heard and taken note of, and was not in any frame of mind to be intimidated by a woman, Queen or not.

His view of kings and queens had changed forever that day when he'd knelt by the side of his dead friend Wulfstan, even *King* Æthelfrith had not challenged him after that, not because he feared Cedric, their relationship was more complex than could possibly be summed up in one word. Cedric spoke to Æthelfrith not as his King, but his equal, all fear of man had died that day his friend, and the woman he'd loved had been murdered. His friend had set honour before any earthly title, and had died for it, now Cedric saw the world through his friend's eyes.

Cedric turned to help Queen Bebba from her horse, but she had already dismounted and was speaking to Prince Eanfrith.

The news of the death of the husband of the two Queens, King Æthelfrith, had reached them but a day past. The shock had struck panic and horror into the hearts of those left at the fortress of Din Guyaroi, fearing the forces of King Edwin.

Æthelfrith's power had rested on his military achievements. His success had now ended emphatically, at the hands of the exiled King Edwin of Deira, who, with the support of King Rædwald of the East Angles, had defeated and killed him in battle at Bawtry by the River Idle in the kingdom of the East Angles.

At first, those left at Din Guyaroi, couldn't or wouldn't believe that the great warrior could have possibly been defeated, but as more and more rumours of the large army coming north began to filter into the fortress, they were forced to believe the unbelievable.

Cedric had been left in command by Æthelfrith. Both knew that the fortress was undermanned. Æthelfrith had taken most of the warriors to face his wife's brother, never imagining the outcome. Cedric was certain he had taken the only option possible for the safety of the Leodwalding line. [5] He knew if they were ever to hope to get their kingdom back they needed to be separated from King Edwin. Otherwise, they would have been part of all manner of family intrigues and possibly even murdered.

Cedric bowed to the two Queens, then glanced round at the faces of the Bebbanburg royal family, *eight*, he mentally calculated. Five were the progeny of Acha, and there was Eanfrith, Æthelfrith's son from his first marriage, who was twenty-six now. Oswiu and Æbbe were Queen Bebba's children. Cedric smiled warmly at Æbbe, she was a special child and he had a soft spot for her. Edric she always called him, she had a habit of shortening names.

Cedric's eyes lingered for a moment longer on Æthelfrith's second child Oswald, who called Acha – Mother. This prince held a place in Cedric's heart, which was his and his alone. Prince Oswald was eleven now, and he was the *double* of his father in every way, even topped off with his black curly hair, *except* that is – for his eyes, they were the gentle soft brown of his mother's and just one glance could warm the coldest heart. His father's eyes had been piercing blue, they could look straight into a man's soul, but Oswald's were the complete opposite they were tender and forgiving.

Oswald would forever be the apple of Cedric's eye; he could not love him more if he had been his *own* son. To Cedric he was perfect in every way, both physically and in his nature. Their eyes met and a smile touched their lips. What was between them passed in that smile, Cedric acknowledged the moment with the slightest nod of his head. He knew he had been more of a father to the boy than Æthelfrith ever had. Æthelfrith was ever too busy being king and he'd left Oswald in his care, *which* was what the gods had always intended. He was a child touched by the gods; Cedric had no doubt of that.

Even though much time had passed – the pain was yet fresh in Cedric's heart, as fresh as the first day he'd lost his friend. Leofwine, Wulfstan's brother, had hanged himself only days after Wulfstan and Aefre's murder. Cedric guessed that he couldn't live with the betrayal of his own kin, his brother, who had loved and cared for him since childhood. Once he'd come to his senses and realised what a wicked thing he'd done, it was too much for him.

Cedric had found him hanging in the stables, but someone else had had to cut him down, Cedric couldn't touch him, even when he was dead. Cedric was filled with disgust. He had never spoken a word to Leofwine after the murder. His utter contempt for his treachery burned like molten lead through his veins, and did yet.

Cedric had once judged his friend Wulfstan and couldn't forgive himself; there was no way he would ever forgive Leofwine for such a despicable act, he would rather rot for eternity in the Hell Mouth.

In Cedric's eyes, Wulfstan was nobler than any man he'd ever known; Wulfstan had understood that his brother, Leofwine, would despise himself once he realised what he'd done, and Wulfstan had told him that he had forgiven him even *before* his act of treachery. Wulfstan knew *full well* – that Leofwine was about to betray him and Aefre, and it would cost them their lives, but such was the nobleness of the friend Cedric loved – that he would forgive *even* their betrayer.

Cedric shook his head at the memory, and he trembled as the pain of that day tore through his limbs afresh – he could *never* understand such forgiveness. Cedric remembered yet his un-abating fury at

Leofwine. If the moment had presented itself, he would have done the work of the rope on Leofwine's neck and strangled him with his bare hands – aye – and gladly.

Oswald had the unsettling feeling that *he* was a part of it.

Oswald yet waited patiently, leaning forward with his arms rested on his knees. After several long minutes, Cedric cleared his throat, straightened his back, and from under thick bushy eyebrows he slowly scanned the group of weary travellers. Most were seated quietly, probably fearfully contemplating the sudden uncertain interruption to their lives.

Cedric coughed once more and gradually began to speak. 'Mmmm, you must be wondering why I beckoned you to my side, my Prince...'

'I assumed that you had something of some importance to say to me, something private perhaps. By the goodwill of the gods I hope that I have not given offence to you in some way.'

'No – you have not wronged me lad, but I have something to say, right enough, then again, at this moment what I have is more something to give.' He began to slowly loosen the leather laces of the package resting on his knee. Oswald looked on, with more and more curiosity. Once Cedric had loosened the binding, he went on to unwrap the oily cloth covering to reveal a magnificent sword, Oswald's eyes widened in amazement.

'By Woden's beard, I've *never* seen such a sword, Cedric. One would only need a glance to know that what is before me is no ordinary sword. Where has it come from? You've never shown me this before.'

'If you are asking where it was given birth, that I cannot tell, for I never knew, perhaps it was a gift from the gods. I do know how it comes to be here on my knee. It was taken from a dead warrior at the battle of Catraeth. The Gododdin came at your father from behind and was about to cleave him in two with a mighty war axe, but your father was too quick for him. In one masterly movement, he spun round and sliced into the warrior's hamstrings just below his mail, the fellow folded into a heap and your father mercifully sent him to his gods.'

'My father, you say? He was the greatest of warriors,' Oswald declared proudly.

'... Aye... *your* father, he was the greatest warrior I have ever seen. None could stand against him.' Cedric glanced away from Oswald's eyes to the sword on his lap.

'What does that word mean,' Oswald asked pointing to the letters on the sword blade, but fearing to touch the mysterious weapon. 'Is it the name of a god? Perhaps the Christ God, look at the crosses at either end of the word.'

'Maybe,' responded Cedric, '*Ulfberht,*' [22] he spoke out the word as he ran the tip of his finger over the embossed letters. 'Though I know naught of the Christian God and never wish to, His followers eat bits of Him is the little I've heard, so there can't be much left now,' Cedric gave a muted chuckle. 'He'll not be much of a challenge to Wōden with half of Him missing,' Oswald smiled too at Cedric's jest. 'What I do know for sure, this is the finest sword I have ever seen, or held.'

'Who did it, or who does it belong to now?'

Cedric hesitated for some time... 'Your father took it and made it his, I was commissioned on his death to make sure it was given to you.'

'Me!'

'If it was my father's it is mine by right.' The voice of Prince Eanfrith came jarringly from behind, soiling this personal moment. Oswald turned to his brother, but Cedric without lifting his head growled.

'When you speak to me *Earsling* – you had better kneel before me, with your head bowed, if you value your life.'

'I – am now your *King*, it is you who will now bow to me.'

There was a moment of deafening silence. 'King or no king, if you are yet standing there when I take my next breath you will have taken your *last* breath. Do you hear me, *boy*?' Cedric said in a fearfully calm voice, but a voice that had the force to burst onto the moment like a jagged shaft of lightning. The energy was more than Eanfrith could stand against and he turned and slunk off muttering to himself. He knew well enough that Cedric might only be a huscarl, but for some unknown reason he held a mysterious position of authority, and no one ever understood why. There was not one, who would dare question him, not even his father King Æthelfrith, who was not only the king but also a respected warrior.

The two were quiet now, while the sudden squall of emotions stilled. Oswald stared at his hands more than a little embarrassed by the interchange. Eanfrith had in fact spoken correctly, in truth, he was their father's eldest and what had belonged to their father was by right his, but *he* was not about to correct Cedric at this moment.

'There is much you do not understand, my Prince. An apple may be red on one side and green on the other, one man sees it as green the other sees it as red. Who tells the truth of it? The truth can be more than we

15

see. I have told you this is your father's sword and it is so; let that be enough for now,' with that odd assertion Cedric passed the sword reverently to Oswald.

Oswald lifted it, felt its balance and then made a play with it slicing through the air. 'This is as you say, like no other sword I have ever felt, my friend. Is it magic?'

'Perhaps it is, it is a sword of honour. It belonged to the most honourable man I have ever known.'

'My father!'

'Aye – *your* father, he called it "Dream World". Ask me no more this day, for what truth I know is mine to know... *for* now. Treasure his gift to you for I fear that today, young as you are, you have become a man, and boy or man, I know you, Prince of Bernicia, will never dishonour your father's trust.'

Oswald stood, slipped his own sword from its frog and replaced it with the Ulfberht. 'What can I say Cedric, I have this precious gift and I will *never* be able to thank my father in person.'

Cedric now rose, faced Oswald and laid his gnarled hand on the boy's shoulder. 'Aye that is a hard thing my son – for me too.'

'Why ever would Father give this prized gift to me above any of his other sons? I cannot but help feel for Eanfrith's hurt.'

'As I have said, for now I will hold my peace. Truths have their season to be told and this is yet winter. When the warmer days come and the time is right, you will know all, I promise you that.'

Oswald frowned at the double talk, but accepted what Cedric said without argument. He knew Cedric to be the bravest and wisest of men – that *truth* – he had *already* harvested.

'But for what comfort it is my son, I know your father would have been proud of you...' Cedric hesitated... 'As *I* am,' and he embraced Oswald.

As Cedric held him, Oswald whispered into his chest, 'I love you my friend.'

Chapter 3

Ad Gefrin

As they rode nearer to Ad Gefrin, Oswald was surprised at the size of the hill fort. It was several years since he'd been there. It was his place of birth and much of his early life had been spent at the palace. He remembered it as being large, but thought that might only be the memory of a child.

Now he saw it was actually even bigger than he remembered.

It was not a fort in the military sense, though it had two timber palisade walls around the perimeter, one inside the other. It was more of a royal palace, a meeting and trading centre for all the local tribes and villages. He remembered that there were four enormous halls, it even had an amphitheatre, and on reflection, he thought that it must have held at least three hundred people or more.

The gates were opened as they neared and the party rode in to be welcomed by anxious slaves and servants rushing hither and thither. Oswald watched Cedric who took a moment to dismount. He leant forward onto the up-stand of his saddle and looked round. Oswald smiled, Cedric never rushed, he was always a man of steady decisions and once he's made up his mind, look out if you stood in his way. To Oswald, Cedric was a hero, he admired everything about him and he would learn all he could from him, whilst he was here. Oswald abruptly clenched his rein tightly at the thought of the inevitability of one day losing his friend. His pony suddenly rebelled at the tightness of the rein, Oswald was conscious of Cedric's eyes upon him and he relaxed his hold and the pony steadied once more. Oswald slipped from the saddle; Cedric was the last to dismount.

Prince Eanfrith was already speaking to someone who appeared to be a man of some note, no doubt asserting his newfound position in the Leodwalding family. Oswald smiled, for he knew how little any title meant at this moment. Cedric's voice was the only voice of importance and Eanfrith would do well to take hold of that truth, and quickly. Oswald knew that Cedric did not suffer fools, not that Eanfrith was a fool, not by any means, but he was no leader either, people were not attracted to him. Whatever the indefinable quality was that drew men to follow and die for another, Eanfrith was not blessed, (or cursed) with such a gift. No matter how Eanfrith wanted men's respect, men never looked to him, in fact Oswald knew the harder he tried the more he was disliked and that saddened him, for like it or not, Eanfrith was in truth, now the head of the Leodwalding family.

Oswald was distracted from his thoughts at the sound of Cedric's voice, 'To me Torem.' Oswald watched as the man talking to Eanfrith bowed to him and went to Cedric and they embraced, plainly he was well known to Cedric. Cedric turned to Oswald and beckoned him to come too. When Oswald neared, Cedric introduced

Torem as an old friend of many years. 'This is the headman, Torem, he has served your family faithfully all his life, Torem this young fellow is Prince Oswald of Bernicia,' Torem bowed and smiled.

'I remember you as a small boy, you have grown since we last met, Lord.' Oswald nodded politely, but he was distracted, he'd glanced at Eanfrith. He could see that he was furious at what he would interpret as a snub by Cedric, but Oswald knew that would not be Cedric's intention, he simply didn't function like that. Cedric was blunt, a man of action not one for the social niceties, he didn't care whether he was liked or not, he didn't seek position or approval of men, or even Queens come to that. Oswald tried to concentrate on what Torem was saying, but he was more concerned as to what Eanfrith was talking to Queen Bebba about. He wondered if their mutterings were their shared disapproval of their head huscarl, not that their displeasure would trouble Cedric in the slightest, nevertheless, what their thoughts and whisperings were about troubled Oswald. He was sure that Cedric lacked wisdom, when dealing with Eanfrith.

Even at his young age, *Oswald* could see that Eanfrith was a young wolf on the prowl, determined to assert himself, and

21

would not forever tolerate those who challenged him. He could well nip at Cedric's heels until he brought him down and Cedric would do well, not to unnecessarily provoke him.

It was by no means certain that Eanfrith would be given the mantle of his father, after all Æthelfrith had not been the direct heir to King Hussa, yet he was made king much to the chagrin of Hussa's son Hering. Eanfrith would yet need to be elected by the Witan. Then there was Queen Bebba; she was cunning, *and* Cedric was entering into their homeland where he would not have the unchallenged power he had enjoyed at Bebbanburg.

A voice broke into the moment, 'Edric,' Princess Æbbe was tugging at Cedric's sword sheath, he looked down and smiled, Æbbe could always draw a smile from Cedric, one of the few who could, Oswald had to concede. Cedric reached down and picked up the child, he even kissed her and she wrapped her arms around his neck.

Cedric turned his attention once more to Torem and made known to him, the predicament in which they now found themselves. Torem was visibly shocked, like everyone else he could not believe that the great King Æthelfrith could, not only be defeated, but also killed. Cedric told him that they would be here no more than two days, but first he needed to find places for the family to sleep and then he was to return to him and he would be given further instruction. Torem bowed and called two men to assist.

Cedric knew they would be safe for a short while, but he also knew they needed to make haste, and be on the way west as quickly as possible. Any small time advantage they had must not be squandered. The now *King* Edwin would come soon enough to stamp his mark on his new kingdom and this palace was a central part of that kingdom.

Oswald saw the royal family being led into the largest of the halls. He remembered it had partitions at either end, which divided the whole area into three. He imagined that Torem would make the most of the two rooms at either end of the hall and see that the queens were separated by the length of the hall, not that Cedric would give such consideration the slightest thought. He did not have time for petty power struggles, as he saw such behaviour. The safety of these royal athelings [6] was his concern, and all that was to happen now would happen at his command. The Leodwalding line would not die out because of his neglect.

'Do you need me Cedric? For if you do not I will go to Mother and see that she has all that she needs. I'm worried about, her she does not look well.'

'You do as you must, Lord. Return to me as soon as you are at peace,' Cedric and Torem bowed to Oswald and he went to seek out his mother. Oswald paused for a moment when he entered the hall, simply to gaze at the size of the space. It was the biggest hall he'd ever been in, there were doorways in each wall. The roof beams were enormous, oak, he guessed, all brightly painted in yellows, greens and reds with serpents and dragons from the underworld. The wattle and daub walls were whitened and they had been painted with hunting scenes. At the far end, there was a raised floor no doubt, where his father and mother would have sat. He wondered, for a moment, if he would be asked to sit there now. He knew Eanfrith would take the centre seat, his mother *and* Queen Bebba would sit either side of him perhaps even Cedric might sit at the high table, but he doubted it, being on show was not Cedric's way. The whole sight before him was quite magnificent, much bigger than their hall at Bebbanburg, but then they were more limited for space on top of the rock. Moreover, there were another two halls almost as big as this, what a place of entertainment and laughter it must have been, but not now, not today.

Oswald shook his head, and returned to his purpose for being there and went to find his mother. She was lying on her bed when he found her and his younger brothers Osguid and Oswudu were there too.

'Where are Oslac, Oslaph and Offa?'

'Fear not son, they are with servants,' Oswald's mother said reassuringly.

'Is there anything I can do for you Mother?' Oswald was concerned, for she did not look well at all.

'No son, you help Cedric. I need to rest and straighten my back after all that riding, no more than that, I'm not as young as you,' and she smiled. 'We will need to move on, we can't stay here too long,' she reached up and drew Oswald near to her. 'Stay close to Cedric whatever happens, Oswald.'

There was a strange intensity in her voice, but he said nothing, he bent down and kissed her, then turned to his brothers. 'You two find our brothers and make sure they come to no harm. I will be with Cedric, Hrodulf and Eanfrith if I am needed. Go now and let Mother rest.'

The next days were spent sourcing all their needs, which could be taken with them, such as ponies, clothing, some food, and tents. There would also be the sharpening and repairing of weapons, all that they would need for the long journey west and the possibility of any subsequent conflict.

In the midst of it all, was Cedric. He, Torem and Hrodulf never seemed to stop. There had been no feast so the question of who sat where never arose.

The few warriors who were at the fort would go with them, as would any who feared the arrival of King Edwin's men. There was some talk of firing the place, but it was decided that it might slow down any pursuers if it was seen to be intact. They may suspect a strong defence of some sort and any time gained would be to their advantage.

It was summer so they could at least hope for good weather and every league west meant greater safety from Edwin. Cedric had been convinced by Eanfrith and Queen Bebba that King Eochaid Buide and his Dalriadan court, at Dunadd would welcome them.

When the last of the travellers walked out of the gate, it was drawn shut and they headed off down the far side of the hill from the now ghostly fort, with the morning sun at their side.

Chapter 4

North West

The only one, with any knowledge of the way to get to Dunadd was Queen Bebba, they all knew that it was northwest of Bebbanburg, or Din Guyaroi as Cedric insisted in calling their home, but no more than that was known.

Their intention was to ride north until they reached the River Abhainn Dubh, [7] the most northerly edge of Æthelfrith's Bernician kingdom, then they would follow the river west past the Roman's most northerly wall, not the one Oswald knew, this wall was much further north, until they reached the western sea.

By the guiding hand of Wōden, they would turn north once more and follow the coast until they reached the kingdom of King Eochaid Buide. With a fair wind, it was thought that the journey would take five or six days. There were families with children walking with them and that would slow them down. They knew it would be dangerous, they might be troubled by all manner of threats; none more worrying than the tribal raiders they might have to face. There were many unfriendly Britons where they were headed, but they had experienced warriors and huscarls with them, they would not be taken easily.

As Cedric contemplated all they might be faced with, he was momentarily distracted as he glanced at Oswald on his pony, riding straight backed with his hand proudly on the pommel of his new sword, in every way he was an atheling. What set him apart, other than his looks, for he was the most handsome of young men with his tanned face and thick mass of curly hair, was how he treated people. He genuinely cared about those lower than himself, even now as they rode, he had the small child of one of the slave girls sitting before him on his pony. He was special, Cedric knew that, and he had pleaded to Wōden to not take him to the "Great Hall" until he'd seen Oswald safe into manhood. Cedric knew Oswald's father and mother would have been proud of him too. He begged the gods that they would tell him the right moment to make such knowledge of his parentage known to him.

It was the afternoon of the third day; they had been travelling for an hour or so since they had rested and eaten. Oswald nudged his pony from his designated place in the line, to Cedric's side.

'We are being followed, Cedric. Look on that ridge to our right, through the pines. I can just make them out,' Oswald said discreetly to Cedric.

'Aye, I see them, Gododdins by the look of their garb. What number do you reckon, son?'

'Twenty, at least, that I can see, possibly more,' Oswald answered, turning to the sound of another rider and seeing Eanfrith coming to them.

'Aye, I'd guess the same,' Cedric said agreeing with Oswald's assessment.

'Is there some problem, Cedric, why have we slowed down?' Eanfrith asked with some irritation. 'Oswald return to your position.'

'Stay with me, son, I need your eyes...'

Oswald looked at his brother; distressed by the awkwardness he always felt when he was the third party between Cedric and Eanfrith. Cedric always gave the impression he didn't like Eanfrith, but Oswald knew Cedric didn't care either way, what annoyed

Cedric, was anyone over-concerned with his or her social position. He related to people on merit not birthright. However, Cedric's challenge to Eanfrith's command, passed without further comment.

'There are some riders on the ridge, to our right, behind the trees, Eanfrith. DON'T stare,' Oswald said more forcefully than he intended as Eanfrith was about to turn his head and look.

'What riders? I haven't seen any riders, you are imagining it,' Eanfrith replied.

'It's not imagined,' Cedric said in a tone that dared Eanfrith to contradict him.

'If it is so, I'll send men to see them off,' Eanfrith said trying to regain some command of the situation.

'Aye, and risk life unnecessarily. You will do no such thing; we know not their number. There may be more men out of our sight. We will wait and watch. For now, *Lord* Eanfrith, ride along our line and see that we close up. Do it without attracting attention, if they think they have the advantage of surprise, we will make – that thought *our* advantage.'

Referring to Eanfrith as *Lord* was sufficient to placate him for now, and he turned his pony and did as he was bidden.

Cedric turned casually and beckoned Hrodulf, with a near imperceptible flick of his head and Hrodulf rode slowly up to them.

'You see them, Hrodulf.'

'Aye, I see them.'

'We will make for that bank yonder afore the river, there is a level sandy place betwixt it and the riverbank, probably made when the river was in spate. We'll need to be careful it might be soft. We'll rest there and wait, with the bank afore us, and the river at the back of us, it'll limit their attacking options. Ride back and ready our warriors for any attack, *no* fuss, Hrodulf.'

Hrodulf turned and made his way to do as he'd been told. Oswald smiled as he watched Hrodulf go about his business. The link he had with Cedric was uncanny, even spiritual. They both thought as one and woe betide anyone who stood against them. Hrodulf was every bit as wily as his old friend Cedric, what they had lost in physical prowess over the years, time having done her relentless work, nibbling slowly away at eyesight, muscles and joints, turning young warriors into old, they more than made up for in experience. The pair had faced every manner of adversary over their years *and* lived to tell the tale, that was enough said.

Oswald knew how fortunate he was to be alongside such warriors and he would watch and learn from them. He saw Eanfrith returning and braced himself for the next moment of confrontation, he wished Eanfrith could recognise the value of having such experienced men around him, and cease forever the constant need to assert himself. Cedric was never going to be cowed by any man merely because of who he was.

Oswald recalled once asking Cedric if he was afraid of *anything*. He'd thought for sometime before he answered, then he said, 'I remember your father once saying to me, before we went to fight the Britons in the kingdom of Powys, west of Mercia, "*You* fear the battle, Cedric, because you hope to live, *I* do not fear the battle because *I hope* to die".'

Oswald recalled how Cedric had frowned as he repeated the conversation... It had obviously troubled him when his father had said it, as it did when he retold it.

It had seemed a sad thing to say. Oswald supposed that Cedric could have meant that his father looked forward to going to dwell with the gods, in the hall of warriors, but something in the way Cedric spoke at the time, had undertones of a wholly darker nature, but Oswald had let it pass.

No more than the undertones of the *current* dilemma, which Oswald focused on once again as Eanfrith returned.

'I have done as you instructed Cedric. What shall I do now?' Oswald breathed a sigh of relief at Eanfrith's welcome deference to Cedric.

'Go to the Queens, your brothers and sister, see that they are protected, and follow us to that riverbank yonder, you see it?'

'Yes.'

'Then have them dismount and take shelter behind it, but do it casually as if we are merely stopping for a rest.'

Eanfrith, nodded, turned and trotted back to the family. Perhaps this is a new Eanfrith thought Oswald, *"Hopefully"*, feeling greatly relieved that another moment of tension had passed them by without confrontation.

The Beast of Bamburgh

No sooner had they dismounted than the Gododdins broke from the cover of the Scotch Pines and charged at them on foot, yelling fearful ear-piercing war cries. They must have noticed the secure position that Cedric had chosen to stop, and decided to attack quickly before they had time to establish themselves.

Little did they know that Cedric's warriors and huscarls were already prepared for the conflict, even now, men were linking their shields to form an impenetrable wooden wall. There was the familiar crash of the metal edges of the large painted lime-wood shields, as they locked together. The screaming Gododdins faltered only for a split second, perhaps surprised by the speed that the shield wall had been assembled before them, but they were committed now and continued unabated.

Oswald stood behind Cedric as he'd been told. He was too young to stand in the shield wall itself, even if he wanted to. Only the strongest and most experienced warriors had that honour. He knew that the men in the wall needed support. For those standing behind the wall there was vital employment, which added to the overall effectiveness of the defence. There was important work for the young, would-be warriors, such as clearing the dead from amongst their feet, or chopping and grabbing at spears that penetrated the wall, as the barricade forged forward.

At the moment of contact, when the two forces came together, the withering shock to the limbs of those in the wall tore through their knotted muscles down their torsos and legs into their feet, hopefully solidly set into the earth, ready to resist the force. The noise was deafening, both sides grunted as one, as the sudden impact forced the air from their lungs.

There was an almost imperceptible hiatus, then more grunts, which were now punctuated by screams as the lethal sharp edges of axe or sword made contact with flesh and bone. The warriors were being bathed in blood sprayed from severed limbs. At first, the Bernicians were outnumbered, but within seconds, the numbers were even. The shieldwall had done its work, and held without losing a single man. Now the Bernicians were pushing forward, the Gododdins were on the back foot trying to resist the energy of the combined force of men linked together. Some of them were tumbling over the bodies of those who had already fallen as they tried to link their shields to offer some credible resistance to this human wall of death, coming remorselessly on to them. It was too late; they had been totally taken aback, thinking they had the irresistible advantage of surprise.

Cedric and Hrodulf were now driving the wall forward at a pace, hacking and slicing as they pushed, which was simply overwhelming the young inexperienced attackers. The handful that were left standing, now turned and ran back to the tree line.

'HOLD,' yelled Cedric and the wall came to a sweating, cursing standstill. Oswald knew Cedric would not give chase in case it was a feint, a ploy, to entrap them, but no, he could see those who'd escaped, mounting their ponies and riding off. The wall now broke and the warriors hacked to death those not already dead. This was the ugly side of victory, which Oswald hated, but he knew that to leave the dying to be tormented by their suffering was far crueller.

'Collect up anything of use, we will take the weapons with us, those dead holding their swords or axes, render them so that they are useless then bury them with the fallen so they might enter the Hell Mouth as noble warriors.'

'They might be *Christians* Cedric,' Oswald said, a little unsure what was the right thing to do.

'Then they will be in for a pleasant surprise when they wake up where people are enjoying themselves, instead of finding that they are with their miserable priest monks, praying to their miserable half eaten god.' That was Cedric's response to Oswald's show of concern, and Cedric laughed, as did those around him. Once the laughter had passed, (Cedric wasn't known for his spontaneous humour, but his description of the Christian afterlife had clearly amused him) he wiped his eyes, put his arm around Oswald and turned to Torem.

'There must be ponies in the wood up there, which belonged to these fellows, fetch them Torem, but take some of these young warriors with you, and watch your back, do you hear?'

'Fear not Cedric, I like life too much, you watch out for your own hide, and I'll watch out for mine,' he replied throwing a lump of dried horse dung at him and laughing, Cedric ducked and laughed too.

They watched Torem go then Oswald and Cedric went down to the river, Cedric yet with his arm around the shoulder of Oswald, to wash the blood from his hands and face the best he could. 'You did well young Oswald of Bernicia, it is important work behind the shieldwall, it can make all the difference in a battle, I'm proud of you, son.'

Oswald always grew a hand's width whenever Cedric praised him; Cedric had that effect on people.

Once Cedric had washed, he made his way to where the queens were sheltered, to reassure them. Cedric quickly explained to the family what he intended to do. They would move off, ford the river as soon as that was possible and travel west on the northern side for it was likely that those who'd escaped the day's conflict would bring others to avenge their defeat. With the help of Hrodulf and Torem, Cedric assembled the travellers and they moved off as quickly as they could, to get clear of the battle site. Once mounted Cedric rode back and forth along the line encouraging and praising his warriors, he seemed in high spirits.

Like all warriors, Cedric was mystically empowered after a battle; so exhilarating was the aftertaste of the conflict. Oswald knew warriors needed that moment of intense excitement, which could only be found on the cusp of life and death. However, for Cedric, underlying and tainting this encounter, was his fear for the Bernician athelings; time was not on their side.

By the time they found a crossing, it was dusk and he was insistent that they crossed over before nightfall. Cedric sent warriors over the crossing ahead of them, and waited uneasily for their signal to enter the water and cross over.

Eventually they returned to the far bank, Hrodulf waved, and beckoned the main party, now they were sure that it was safe. Cedric was last to cross, he made certain that all were safely to the other side, he took one last look back over the road they'd travelled then nudged his pony forward into the cold, fast flowing, brackish water.

They camped on a derelict farm holding that night, Oswald slept lightly, as most of them did. Every time he stirred and glanced over to where Cedric had laid out his bed rug, he saw that Cedric was awake walking back and forth along the perimeter of the camp, stopping every few steps to stare out into the darkness.

They were well beyond the kingdom of Bernicia now; every step was measured in the pounding heartbeats of the warriors. They knew that they could be attacked and overwhelmed at any moment. Though they were able men, their numbers were few, too few to venture into an enemies heartland with impunity.

When they neared Dunadd, the plan was that they would send a rider to meet King Eochaid Buide at the Dalriadan court; perhaps Prince Eanfrith himself would go because of his mother's connection to King Eochaid. Queen Bebba had a ring he would recognise, and the rider would give it to him.

Cedric tried, but he could not convince himself that this was a wise plan, but he could not think of a better one. Even if the royal family were saved, because of their kinship, King Eochaid Buide might still have the men murdered for his own safety. Cedric thought that he would be happy just to know the family were safe, his life was theirs so what did it matter.

Oswald was pleased to see his mother Queen Acha looking better, she hadn't looked well of late, some malady of her gut, he'd been told. Eanfrith had been kind to her, for she had been his mother too since he was, thirteen or so, Oswald reckoned. He wasn't quite sure when his father and mother were married, he must ask her or Cedric, he'd never thought about it before.

There would be no fires this night, but it was a warm night so it was no hardship to them.

Chapter 5

Dunadd

The Bernicians were now on the borders of Dalriada, and so were at this moment in even greater danger from attack. Cedric decided that they would camp in a large rocky outcrop on the side of a valley. They would not be easily seen and yet they would have a good view of the surrounding vicinity. He knew that it was far from

42

perfect as a defensive position, but they would have to make the best of it.

Oswald was thankful that there had not been any more conflict between Cedric and Eanfrith.

When Eanfrith had announced that he would be the one to approach King Eochaid Buide, at the Dalriadan court, Cedric said nothing. Hrodulf would go with him and two more huscarls; the two queens and their children would wait where they were. Queen Bebba told Cedric that it was less than a day's ride to the hill fort of Dunadd. If Wōden were with them, Eanfrith would return before nightfall.

'Take care Hrodulf,' Cedric said quietly to him, 'and keep a tight rein on the young hothead. As much as he annoys me, he is brave enough to do this. It's his arrogance, which is his downfall. Talk to him on the way, try to steady his natural tendency to act rashly, so that he doesn't end up without his stupid head.'

'Fear not Cedric, I will watch out for him, we will be back before nightfall.' With that, Eanfrith gave the order to move off.

They watched the small group ride away and Cedric turned to Oswald. 'That's it for now, young Oswald, all we can do is wait and hope that the gods are on our side.'

'Do you think that King Eochaid Buide will look favourably on us, Cedric?'

'Queen Bebba seems certain that he will, I'm sure she knows best,' Cedric was trying to reassure his young prince, and he hoped that he sounded more confident than he felt. It was out of his hands now and solely down to the benevolence of the gods.

Cedric leant casually against a large pine chewing on a stalk of grass, and staring in the direction of Dunadd. He'd been standing alone for most of the day. It was mid-afternoon when he suddenly pushed himself from the tree trunk and stood erect with his hand mindlessly flexing around the pommel of his sword.

'Ready yourselves men,' he turned and called to the warriors relaxing around the camp. He had spotted riders, he couldn't yet be certain if it was Eanfrith or not, There were about twenty in total, both Oswald and Torem came to his side.

'Is it Eanfrith?' asked Oswald.

'You tell *me*, I can't make any of them out, but they've turned this way and are definitely coming towards our position.'

'YES, it's Eanfrith and our men.'

'Is Hrodulf with them?'

'Yes, and others, I do not recognise, there seems to be a boy with them.'

'A *boy*!'

They watched intently as the riders drew ever closer. There was indeed a young boy with them much the same age as Oswald.

The group stopped half a league short of the forest. Eanfrith and the boy separated from the group and rode on towards them.

'*Eanfrith*,' Oswald called with genuine delight at seeing his brother, safely returned.

'Oswald, Cedric,' Cedric gave a curt nod of his head. 'This is Prince Domnall Brecc, son of the great King Eochaid. King Eochaid has send his son, Prince Domnall, in good faith, to show that we are welcome and need have no fear.'

Queen Bebba now approached them, Eanfrith glanced to her and smiled, 'King Eochaid looks forward to seeing you once more, my Lady.'

She smiled too, 'Thank you Eanfrith. You are a fine young man now, Prince Domnall, do you remember me?'

The boy smiled and spoke for the first time, bowing, 'I'm sorry, I do not, but I know *of* you, you must be Queen Bebba. My father has spoken of you often, clearly he

45

thinks highly of you, he sends his greetings to you and all the Bernician family.'

Queen Bebba was clearly delighted; she reached up and affectionately squeezed his hand.

'You have done well, Lord Eanfrith,' Cedric said with some generosity of spirit.

'Thank you Cedric, King Eochaid is expecting us to return before dark, so we will need to make haste, are we ready to go?'

'Yes, we did not unpack the animals, all we need to do is mount up and follow you.' With that Cedric gestured and those waiting, mounted. Eanfrith turned his pony and took the lead followed by Prince Domnall.

Cedric was quite happy to drop behind; first, to be sure Queen Acha was not too fearful. Once he was satisfied that she was at peace he went to speak to Hrodulf.

'What did you make of this King Eochaid, then, Hrodulf?'

'He seemed very friendly, I liked him, he's well past the flush of youth, maybe... in his early thirties, is my guess. He has a head of long thick fair hair, hence his name, Eochaid *Buide*. The lad's only ten,' Hrodulf nodded in the direction of Prince Domnall Brecc. 'I asked him his age as we rode here. I thought it an opportunity to learn what I could. He speaks Saxon well enough. He has a sister; she's eleven and has the makings of a fine beauty. The lad's called Domnall Brecc, because of his freckles, so he told me.'

'Aye, he has a rare ginger mop right enough,' smiled Cedric.

The conversation with Hrodulf put Cedric at ease. Perhaps all that Queen Bebba said would be, is exactly how it was, thanks be to the gods.

It was dark by the time they reached the hill fort of Dunadd, [10] but it was clear to Oswald that it was more of a fort than Ad Gefrin. There were fortified earth mounds within the stockade with many dwellings and places of work. The earthen mounds were at one end, there were several, one on top of the other, with deep ditches around each mound. At the summit, there was a large flat area with a longhouse and several smaller buildings. They rode onto the first raised area and stopped; Oswald assumed that at the top was the dwelling place of King Eochaid. It was not unlike Bebbanburg, a rocky hill set in the earth, a place that stood out in the landscape. A

47

position well suited to give visible status and authority to any king.

They dismounted and servants took their ponies. As they were led on foot, up the steep inclines, and through the narrow entrances to each level, Oswald took his mother's arm and she smiled at his kindness. There were three raised mounds in all. At the top, they were taken into the large imposing longhouse. Cedric was the last to enter. There were several people seated at a long table at the far end of the hall, on a raised platform. All this seemed familiar to Oswald; it was much the same as any other longhouse. Oswald assumed the man seated at the long table was King Eochaid, who, on seeing them enter, rose to his feet, stepped from the platform and came towards them, his arms outstretched in welcome.

The two Queens were greeted warmly. He embraced Queen Bebba first, then he bowed to Queen Acha and embraced her too, with equal kindness, and then he embraced Eanfrith.

Oswald thought him a very pleasant individual although he was struggling to make out much of what he said. One by one, Æthelfrith's family were introduced to the King and they each in turn bowed. There was a slender very beautiful young girl

48

standing on the dais, who caught Oswald's eye, and they exchanged smiles, he thought that she must be the princess that he'd heard Hrodulf mention to Cedric.

The Queens were seated on the dais next to King Eochaid, and his son. Oswald, his brothers and sister were seated just below them, but still in a place of honour. He sat next to Offa with his other siblings between him and Oswiu. Each time Oswald glanced up at the princess, she smiled at him. He thought, if this was to be the welcome they were to receive he was feeling very welcomed indeed.

However, he doubted that Cedric felt the same. He was seated next to one of their priest monks, and, if his facial expression was to be the measure, he didn't seem to be enjoying the experience. Oswald couldn't help noticing the priest monk's unusual baldhead. He was compelled to smile at Cedric's obvious discomfort.

The mete was better than they had had for days, but not what he'd describe as a feast and there were foods of which he was unfamiliar. He was sure if they had been expected, King Eochaid would have done more to impress them.

After they'd eaten, while he was speaking to Oswiu, a hand tapped his shoulder and he turned to the smiling face of the princess from the high table.

She bowed and he responded in like manner. She was obviously offering a welcome of some sort, but his knowledge of her language was limited to the few words he'd learned from Queen Bebba on the journey here. He established that her name was Helen, an unfamiliar name to him; it did not trip off his tongue easily. He hoped that she understood that he was called Oswald, the second son of the famed King Æthelfrith of Bernicia. All the while he tried to talk to her she smiled. She actually spoke more of his Saxon than the miserable few words he'd managed to speak of her Hibernian, if that's what it was. She said that she'd been taught by their holy people, and that *they* were all learned men.

Whatever language it was, it was pleasing to the ear, soft and easy to listen to, almost musical. The pleasant few moments were interrupted by Cedric, Oswald introduced Princess Helen to him and he smiled and bowed. Cedric told him that he was going to be shown where his men were to stay, by a Briton warrior of some authority and asked if Oswald was content to wait in the hall until he returned. The Princess said she would show Prince Oswald where he and his family were to sleep. Cedric hesitated for a moment, bowed, and left.

The Princess took Oswald's hand and led him out of the hall to another building, which was being cleared. She showed him where Queen Bebba would be housed and yet another roundhouse where Queen Acha and *her* servants would sleep.

Oswald asked her where her mother, the Queen, was. The smile slipped slowly from her face, she lowered her eyes, and there was a moment before she spoke. Eventually, she said in a soft whisper that her mother had died when her brother Prince Domnall was born.

'I can barely remember her. My one lasting memory of her is the warm comfort of snuggling into her hair.'

Oswald told her how sorry he was, Helen said that her father had told her this day that his mother was also dead, killed when he was a baby.

Oswald drew his head back, stunned; unsure he'd understood her. It was now his turn to be slow to respond.

'No, no – my mother is not dead she is Queen Acha. You must mean my *half* brother Eanfrith, *his* mother is dead.'

'Oh... no, not Prince Eanfrith, his mother was well known to my father, she died many years ago. I was told your mother was

Queen Aefre, Queen Acha's sister and she was killed in some fearful accident.'

Oswald could only stare vacantly at her; he didn't know what to say. *Slowly* – little scraps of things that had been said over the years took on a completely different shade, and shape... he was speechless. He'd never heard of a Queen called Aefre, what was this girl saying? Aefre, Aefre, he'd never even heard the name before, as far as he could recall. Then somewhere in the fog of the past he recalled a servant called Rowena, *yes...* Rowena, that was her name. She was always especially kind to him, yes Rowena, he remembered her now. She was combing his hair, and said that the comb was very special to her; it had belonged to her Lady Aefre whom she had loved... yes, he was sure that was the name, Aefre.

'*Aefre,*' he spoke the name out loud.

'Perhaps, I misunderstood, or my father was mistaken,' she suggested gently, seeing the distress suddenly transforming Oswald's face. 'I'm sorry if I have caused you some pain, Oswald.'

Oswald hadn't heard her.

'I'm *sorry* Prince Oswald,' she said once more.

'Oh... yes, yes, no, it's nothing don't be troubled, a trivial misunderstanding.'

It was black dark now, though the hilltop was well supplied with flaming torches, it was yet difficult to see, as if the darkness swallowed up the light, and with it, all he believed was his past.

Oswald needed to find Cedric; his head was in turmoil, he couldn't think straight. This innocent young princess had unsettled him more than she could ever imagine. He asked her if she knew where Cedric might be, she pointed to one of the larger roundhouses, and he thanked her for her kindness, in making their new home known to him. He said he would walk back to the main hall with her and then go to his friend; she nodded yet feeling that she had without intention, hurt this gentle young prince.

Chapter 6

Revelation

Oswald literally stumbled into the roundhouse where Princess Helen had told him Cedric would be. He leant against one of the posts supporting the rafters, pressed his head back against the rough wood, closed his eyes, and tried to collect

54

himself. Princess Helen's revelation had disturbed him to the point that he could hardly function; he could barely put one foot in front of the other, never mind think.

Cedric didn't see him at first; *he* was talking to a Dalriadan warrior, a Briton from the southern kingdom of Pengwern. A Wealas [11] man called Daffyd whose arms were beautifully decorated with lavishly coloured tattoos of twisted serpents and animals from the underworld, worked into eternal knots. [14] Cedric had never seen such fine workmanship, and was fascinated. When he glanced up, he caught sight of Oswald and he was immediately alarmed by the look of utter anguish on his face.

That was the end of any social pleasantry for Cedric. His conversation with Daffyd ended abruptly, it was no longer possible for him to continue talking to the Briton; he was too distracted by his concern for Oswald. He offered his paltry excuses to Daffyd and made his way *fearfully* to where Oswald was slumped awkwardly against the roundhouse frame. Cedric's hand gripped the pommel of his sword and his eyes scanned his surroundings for any sign of threat as he neared Oswald.

Oswald was clearly distressed, Cedric glanced to the entrance; he'd not heard any disruption outside. Oswald didn't appear injured in any way and yet he was obviously disturbed. Oswald seemed to be unaware that Cedric was now standing in front of him. Cedric laid his hand lightly on his shoulder.

'What has happened, son? Are you hurt?'

Oswald's eyes gradually rose to meet Cedric's and he slowly shook his head. 'I don't rightly know.'

'What do you mean? Speak plainly boy, not in riddles.' This sort of confused speech was not how Cedric's thought world worked.

Cedric was a man of clear thought, a decision maker; he didn't spend his days in tortured anguish over relationships, like some lovesick scop [12]. He did what he thought was right and honourable and that was that, take it or leave it. Either he liked a person or he didn't and expected no more from anyone else, *but...* it was so different when it came to Oswald. Their relationship contradicted everything that was Cedric, and he was rendered maddeningly helpless before it.

Oswald did no more than slowly shake his head at Cedric's question.

'Come boy, we will sit by that pile of skins yonder,' Cedric said in a whisper, taking Oswald's arm, and leading him into the darkness, where he bade him sit. 'You were smiling, a young man very pleased when I left you, but a short while since. This is not the face of a man flattered by the attention of a beautiful young princess,' Cedric said, floundering out of his depth, and attempting to lighten the moment, *without success*. 'Do you wish to tell me what ails you, or do you desire your own company, I will afford you either?' His voice now had more than a hint of irritation.

Oswald again shook his head despondently and Cedric made to rise, but Oswald touched Cedric's arm and he relaxed once more onto the ground.

'I don't know what to say, Cedric... The *princess* – told me the strangest tale and I know not the truth of it, but it had the echo of things past and stirred up scraps of half memories which were sleeping, ready for such a moment to awaken.'

'Mmm... you are yet speaking in riddles I ask again, *speak* plainly boy,' Cedric asserted, perturbed and unsettled by the tone of Oswald's voice. 'Do you want to share these awakened memories or not, if you wish me to offer some help, speak clearly? Perhaps I can cast some light on what ails you.'

Oswald stared at Cedric for some time as if daring himself to open the secret box and find out what was inside...

'Who... was... my *mother*, Cedric?'

Cedric felt the blood draining from his head down his spine, out through his backside and into the dirt floor, and was mightily thankful he was at this moment seated. The roundhouse was suddenly a spinning empty space, a void, a timeless hole; the only sound was the pounding pulse in his head. Before he could even attempt to answer Oswald's question, Oswald spoke once more.

'The princess said my mother was called Aefre, and she'd been killed when I was a baby, what do you know of the truth of this?'

The only movement on Cedric's expressionless face was his flexing jaw muscles. He was struck dumb; no words would form on his tongue. Oswald was staring at him now. Cedric could only look at Oswald out of the corner of his eye. He ran his dried out tongue over his parched lips and cleared his throat, in a vain attempt to give life to some response, *and* still Oswald stared at him.

Anything but this, whatever could he say... this was the question he ever feared, what – *should* – he say? Cedric knew he would swear and lie his way into the Hell Mouth for this boy, aye and willingly, but could he lie – *to* – him?

What *was* the truth? Oswald was a bastard, and would be an outcast, no place for him in the royal family. The world would cast him into the outer darkness of the wandering spirits who had nowhere to rest their heads. He'd be no more than a shallow breath in the never-ending story of memories past.

Cedric was sure that no one knew the true story, suspected, yes. He was only too aware of the gossip that had been spread far and wide by the toad of toads, Lord Hering. Cedric had removed the head of that earsling and affixed it onto a spear shaft driven into the middle of the courtyard at Din Guyaroi, so that all might see the end that honour served out to traitors. The *rumour* had been mete and drink to those who yearned to undermine King Æthelfrith.

Cedric would have rubbished such a story, and had many times, but this was different. Was he to taint this precious relationship with lies? He filled his lungs and breathed out slowly, just as he would when facing any giant.

'...The princess...' he cleared his throat once more, 'speaks the truth...' the words fell from his lips like rotten clay. Oswald never flinched. 'Your birth mother... was the sister of Queen Acha. She was called by the name of Aefre and married to King Æthelfrith... *but* she was in love with your father and had been from the moment they met.'

'*My father* what do you mean? King Æthelfrith was – is my father.'

'I'm sorry son, but your real *father* was my Lord and friend, though I was never worthy of his friendship. He was so far above me in every way. He was Lord Wulfstan, the bravest and most noble warrior there ever was, or ever will be. An example to all and loved by all, but none more than me, save your mother.'

'I don't understand, Cedric. "*The* great Wulfstan", all talk of him, but King Æthelfrith always treated me as his son, and I called *him* Father.'

Cedric was again quiet for some moments; he hung his head and rubbed his face with his hand. 'I alone know the truth of this, others may have suspected, but none spoke of their suspicions for fear of what I may do to them. In that, they were wise, for I would have sent them straight to the Hell Mouth, if they had uttered a single word of their doubts.'

Oswald hardly breathed as Cedric spoke.

'King Æthelfrith chose to believe you were his son, if he ever suspected differently I know not, for no such doubts were ever breathed or made known to me, and I was content with that.'

'But what happened to them, this Aefre, and this Wulfstan?'

'Their love was such a love that is given by the gods to only a very few. A love which is not quenched by death, an eternal love, the like of which I have never seen before or since. They were betrayed by a man, with the name of all that is wicked, and then murdered. Neither offered any defence and died in each other's arms, robbed of life by the hand of treachery. Your father's last words were for you and you now hold fast to his hand when you grip his sword. There was his helma too, the most beautiful helma you could ever imagine. I have never seen its like afore or since. It was made to look like a fearsome face, it had two golden winged dragons over the crown, their wings formed the eyebrows of the helma, and they were mounted with blood red garnets. The cheeks and the face guard were engraved with mystical scenes. Aye... it was terrible thing to behold. On seeing it, men trembled with fear, for they thought that they were faced with a warrior from the spirit world. King Æthelfrith took it after your father's death, but I kept your father's sword, it was his dying command, that it should be given to you and that I have done. King Rædwald no doubt has the helma [20] now, the ill begotten spawn. Might it be affixed to his head forever in the spirit world where all that is unworthy dwells.' Cedric turned to Oswald, saw the tears streaming down his face and he drew him into his arms. Neither spoke for several minutes.

'Does my mother know of this?' Oswald asked drawing his forearm across his eyes to wipe away the tears.

'I don't know what she knows except that you are not hers, but her sister, Queen Aefre's child. I think that your real mother's maid knew the truth of it, they were very close, but she never talked of it. She is dead now, she was a brave loyal woman. I fancy that she suffered some lasting injury when she was captured by the Gododdins who dragged her behind their horses, then hung her by her wrist. Your mother and father risked all to rescue her. Hrodulf will tell you of their bravery, he was there, and he too owes his life to them. They were not like the rest of us, all who knew them would die for them, aye and willingly.'

'Was this maid called Rowena?'

Cedric was for a moment startled by Oswald's knowledge, 'Aye, *Rowena*, that was her name. She nursed you when you were young, until she died. I do know that Queen Acha, whom you know as mother, has loved you as her own, and I'm forever thankful for that. She is a good woman and a good mother.'

Both Cedric and Oswald now sat silently with their heads hung between raised knees.

'Why have you never told me this before, Cedric, I had the right to know?'

Cedric raised his head, narrowed his eyes and stared across the smoky air of the roundhouse.

'Aye... no doubt you had, and I would have told you, believe me, but there has been enough pain wrapped up in this tale to last a hundred lifetimes and more. Try to understand that these people that we're speaking of, are merely names to you at this moment, yes, by the gods, important names I grant you, but only names nevertheless, *but* they were real living breathing people whom *I* knew, and loved. You can never hear your father's voice, or your mother's laughter, *I can,* and I carry the pain and guilt every day.'

'Why do *you* carry any guilt? Any such guilt that there was, was surely not yours to bear.'

'You think not do you? If I hadn't been such a blind fool, I could have done something to save your mother and father, they need not have died and that is a hellish load for a man the likes of me to carry, believe me son.'

'Is that really what you believe? Is it not the gods in the end, who decide whether we live or die? That's what *you* would say to me, or do the gods have different ways when it comes to you? If they were truly my mother and father, as you say, in their name I absolve you of any guilt.'

Cedric lifted his head and stared at Oswald for some moments, tears filled his eyes, and he leant forward, reached out his trembling hand, and touched Oswald's knee. Oswald had never seen this side of Cedric and it humbled him to see this great man, whom he loved, so broken.

They sat in silence for some time until Oswald whispered, 'I want you to tell me everything about these two people Cedric; perhaps you are the only person who can.'

'Aye, perhaps I am,' he answered in a sad uneven voice.

'But not now, I must walk in the dark alone and think on all that has been made known to me. Thank you Cedric; do not chastise yourself for any neglect. This changes nothing between us, if *anything*, the bond has tightened.'

'Aye, I know son, I am bound to you for life, naught but death will separate my heart from yours,' Cedric formed a sad smile on his lips and gave a sharp nod of his head.

Oswald stood and walked from the roundhouse leaving Cedric sitting in the shadows, staring blindly up to the rafters.

Iona Cathedral

Chapter 7

A Future Decided

Oswald had slept little over the last few days and this night was no different. Whenever he glanced over to his brothers, they were sleeping; all was quiet. The only light was the glow from the dying embers of the fire and it touched the edges of their sleeping faces.

Time and again, fear swept over him in waves of uncertainty. Those around him were uncertain about their future, but *he* wasn't even certain about the past. All he had ever known and believed to be true about his self had been turned upside down.

He stared at Oswiu, who lay nearby him, of all his brothers, Oswald always felt closest to him, though he was almost seven years Oswald's junior. Perhaps it was because he'd always looked after Oswiu, he had cared for him since he'd been a toddler; they'd always had some deeper connection. However, these were – *not* – his brothers not even his *half-brothers*, he was in *no way* linked by blood to anything of King Æthelfrith, whom he'd always known as Father.

If what Cedric had told him was the truth, his mother was his aunt and the man now on the throne of Bernicia, King Edwin who was his uncle, was more his relative than those he'd always known as his nearest kin. He had no birthrights within this family who were sleeping so soundly around him. He could even be seen as a threat, a danger, as the nephew of the usurper Edwin. Eanfrith of all his brothers would probably hate him. He had never been close to Eanfrith who was now, at the very least, "Head" of the family.

Oswald knew that over the years, they had done no more than tolerate each other. He had always thought Eanfrith a very plain man, lacking any colour, and with not much imagination, they had little in common. Eanfrith was forever obsessed about people respecting him and acknowledging who he was, but this obsession had the opposite effect on people and they respected him less.

Oswald stared once more into the gloom of the smoke-blackened rafters and sighed; perhaps Cedric was mistaken. He couldn't know for a fact that he was not the son of King Æthelfrith. Oswald knew that Cedric would never intentionally lie to him, *no*, for Cedric to lie to him was inconceivable. It was obvious how much it had cost Cedric to make such a thing known to him, but he *might* have been mistaken. Because Cedric believed it to be the truth, it did not mean that it was the truth. Would it now be right to make such known to all, and cause hurt to those he loved by telling this uncertain truth? On the other hand, was he saying this to himself as a way of merely pouring salve on his conscience, if he kept this information secret? If he kept the secret, his life would suffer no disruption and he would retain his position without question, but could he live with such a lie? This was impossible, he would have to talk to Cedric once more and tell him how confused he was and seek his advice about what he should do.

Since Cedric had made this nightmare known to Oswald, it had not been mentioned again, but their times together had become strained.

Oswald thought, perhaps this was why Cedric had said naught to me all these years, he had known what turmoil such knowledge would cause in my thought world and he wanted to spare me.

Oswald awoke to the noise and chatter of his brothers rising to the new day, whilst *he* felt as if he had only just fallen asleep. The very last thing he needed this day was his sister Æbbe jumping on him.

'Cuddle, Swald,' she giggled.

'Why are you not with your mother?' He asked her rubbing his eyes.

'I wanted to see you.'

'Well, aren't *I* the blest one,' he said unconvincingly, whilst hugging and kissing her. 'Leave me, you child of Eostre [13] and I will wash and ready myself, then I will see you in the main hall when we eat. Off you go.' With that, Æbbe jumped up and ran out the door. Oswald sat up yawned and stretched then promptly fell back on his bed.

'Cedric came in earlier to see you, but you were yet asleep,' Oswiu called across to him as he was leaving the roundhouse.

'Did he say what he wanted?' asked Oswald raising himself onto his elbows.

'No, he said that he would see you in the hall when you went for the morning's mete.'

Oswald raised himself, and went to the half barrel filled with water for them to wash in. He submerged his head in the cold water, withdrew it, shook it vigorously, like a dog coming out of a river, and dried his face on a cloth. He was startled as a hand slipped round his shoulder and he spontaneously shivered.

'Cedric – you surprised me. I was told that you would be in the hall.'

'Yes, I was, but I was unable to settle and came once more to see if you'd yet stirred. I am concerned. We have been avoiding the things which are on our minds.'

'I know, I'm sorry, but I need time to let all you have made known to me take a proper place in my life. Unless that is, you have something else pressing of which you wish to speak.'

'No, nothing that will change what I have already said, as long as you know that I am here for you, if you want to ask me questions.'

'Forgive me Cedric. It's not that I am avoiding you in any way; it's simply that I do not know what I should, or want, to know. This might take some time to find a place of rest in my head, before I can have any clear questions.'

'I always knew what confusion it would bring, that said, let it be no obstacle between us. Come, join me in the hall, if it is your wish.'

Oswald nodded, 'Thank you, Cedric, as always, I know your friendship and counsel to be sound,' and Cedric wrapped his arm around Oswald's shoulder and they made their way to the hall.

Oswald knew that he was late, the hall was full, but they found a place to sit, some had already eaten and were leaving. The settlement was even now busy with the days work.

As soon as Æbbe saw him, she ran to him and climbed onto his lap. Whilst Oswald and Cedric were eating, a servant came to them, bowed and informed Oswald that King Eochaid Buide wanted to speak with him.

'Now?'

'Yes, Lord.' Oswald turned to Cedric; Cedric could only lift his hands and shrug.

Oswald set Æbbe onto the ground, rose from his bench and followed the servant.

King Eochaid Buide smiled as Oswald approached. Queen Acha, Queen Bebba, Prince Domnall, Eanfrith and Helen were sitting with him; Oswald noticed Eanfrith's severe countenance. The King gestured with a sweep of his hand for Oswald to be seated; Oswald bowed and took the seat offered. King Eochaid Buide looked to Queen Bebba.

'The King has asked me to speak for him, his grasp of Saxon is limited.' Oswald nodded to the King. 'The King wants you to go to an island nearby to learn from the monks who live there. They will teach you to read, write, and speak Hibernian so that you will be more able to converse with him, and his people.'

Oswald was silent as he thought about what she said. What did she mean, go to an island, was that to live there, *forever*?

Queen Bebba waited a moment for Oswald to respond, then, continued, 'You will not be alone, Eanfrith and Oswiu will go too, as will your other brothers when they are older, we spoke to them before you came into the hall. The King thinks such learning is vitally important for all young athelings.'

'Will *you* come with us Mother?' Oswald asked Queen Acha.

She shook her head and Queen Bebba answered for her. 'No, they do not allow any women on the island, but your mother, the Queen will be nearby on the island of Coll, it's not far from the island of Iona, where you will be, so you will be able to visit her often.'

'Is this your wish, Mother?'

At last, his mother did speak, 'I think that it will be for the best Oswald. I will have my own people with me on the island and will be independent, it is very considerate of the King to think about my feelings, and as Queen Bebba says, you will be able to come often to see me.'

'What of Cedric?'

'He will go with me, and be my lead huscarl, as he has always been.'

'If it is your wish Mother, I will do as you advise.'

Queen Bebba, then spoke to King Eochaid Buide and he smiled at Oswald. Oswald supposed that she was telling King Eochaid what he had said.

'You will learn much,' the King offered, speaking in his faltering Saxon.

'The King has told me that you may do as you wish while you are in Dunadd. He hopes that you like your new home, for he

73

says it will be your home for as long as you need it to be. *Eanfrith*,' Queen Bebba said turning to Eanfrith, 'you might think it necessary to talk with your brother; perhaps you could walk with Oswald and reassure him.'

Eanfrith stood up and beckoned Oswald as he stepped abruptly from the raised platform. Oswald glanced once more at Queen Acha and then followed Eanfrith who was clearly not enthralled by the proposals for their future.

As they walked from the hall Oswald could see Cedric watching, and didn't want to leave without speaking to him.

'One moment, Eanfrith,' Oswald said tugging on Eanfrith's sleeve. 'I must speak to Cedric and tell him what was said to us by the King.' Cedric watched suspiciously as they came to him. Oswald sat next to him in the place he had moments since vacated, fortunately Æbbe had run off to lavish her attention on someone more disposed to entertain her.

'What has been said then?' Cedric asked with some reservation.

Oswald repeated what he'd been told. Cedric looked to Eanfrith for confirmation and he nodded his agreement.

'When will these things happen?' Cedric asked Eanfrith.

'As soon as possible, two, three days perhaps,' Eanfrith answered with undisguised agitation.

'I can see benefits to learning the things that these people know, Cedric. What is there to lose and much to gain?'

'Mmm,' was all Cedric would say.

Eanfrith and Oswald walked in silence for some time before Oswald had cleared a place in his mind and was able to say what had assembled in the space. 'Perhaps this is a good thing, Eanfrith.'

'You're a fool, they want to make us be and think like them, then they will use us for their own ends.'

Oswald was surprised at Eanfrith's tone, 'I thought that you had *agreed* to do this!'

'I had no choice, but I will never be like them.'

'But these are your relatives.'

'I am a Bernician and a King, *that* comes first. I will not be robbed of my inheritance. As soon as I can I will drive the usurper, *your* mother's brother, from my kingdom.'

Oswald was confused now; Eanfrith was all but making him chose between him and his mother. They continued on in silence, walking round the timber stockade until they returned to where they'd started, having said very little of consequence. Whatever Eanfrith said, Oswald was determined that he would make as much as he could from the opportunity, besides he was curious about this god that his followers ate. He wondered if it was a bit like holding his father's sword. His father was in the sword and by holding it he became in some mystical way, an extension of his father. Perhaps this god eating was more symbolic and it made those who did this, figuratively part of their god.

'I will leave you now Oswald, I need to make myself known to the smith, think on what we have said. Don't forget who you are, or who I am, remember I am your king, *not* King Eochaid Buide.'

Who *am I*? I no longer know... Oswald thought to himself... I will go to this island and learn all I can from these monks. I will make it my strength not my weakness.

'*Prince Oswald!*' a voice suddenly forced its way unceremoniously into his world of thought.

Oswald instinctively looked up and smiled as he saw Princess Helen coming towards him.

'Hello,' he replied smiling, 'I'm sorry, I was deep in thought.

'You are always thinking, I leave such an occupation to my elders, come, would you like to ride outside the fort? I will show you some of my favourite places. If you are leaving for a while I would like you to remember me, *perhaps* "Sometime", when you are not so busy with your thinking,' she laughed and poked him with her finger, making Oswald laugh too. She was one of those people who brought laughter with her wherever she went. There was something clean and innocent about her, he thought and smiled.

'I'm sure I will remember you. Will it be *safe* to ride alone outside the fort?'

'Oh, we will not go far from the fort, Father would be furious.'

'In that case I would like that very much.'

The princess took him to the stables and two ponies were saddled for them.

They gently walked their ponies and talked without losing sight of the fort, Oswald made sure of that.

'Helen is a name I am unfamiliar with, Princess.'

She smiled, '...we have many traders who come here from far-off lands to sell their wares. My brooch,' she pointed to the beautiful silver pennanular brooch securing her cloak. 'These stones are called garnets and they come from a land that is so far away, it is in another world.'

'I wonder where that is? Your brooch is very beautiful.'

'Thank you, I think so too. My father bought it for my mother, from a trader who told a wonderful story of a beautiful young princess from his land, called Helen. She was so beautiful that all men wanted her for their wife. It is a very complicated story with much intrigue but she was kidnapped and held in a fort made of stone, even bigger than Dunadd. The bit I like best is where those who came to rescue her pretend to leave, and hid in the belly of a great wooden horse they'd made. The people dragged the horse into their fort, they didn't know about the warriors inside. At night, the warriors came out of the wooden horse, conquered the fort and rescued Helen.'

'And what happened to her in the end?'

'It was a sad end, I'm afraid. She went to live with someone she thought a friend, a woman called Polyxo.' Oswald drew back his head at the odd name.

'I have never heard of that name either, it's not so easy to say as Helen.'

'The story is filled with strange names from this far-off land,' Helen laughed. 'This woman Polyxo, actually hated Helen, blaming her for the death of her husband who had been killed in the wars, and she wanted revenge, to that end she pretended to like Helen. One night when Helen was bathing she was tricked by the woman, taken and hanged.'

'That is indeed a sad tale, may the gods have prepared a life of only happiness for *you*, Helen.'

'Ha, my mother loved the story and she liked the name Helen so much, she made it my name. Perhaps the trader will come again this year and he will tell it once more.'

'Do you know, I *will* miss you, Princess Helen.'

Chapter 8

Journey to Iona

It was a fresh autumn morning as they made their way to the shore and the four awaiting boats; someone said they were called curraghs. [15] On nearing the craft, Oswald was somewhat concerned, for they appeared very flimsy indeed.

At first glance, they seemed to be no more than a light wooden frame covered with either cloth or skins and coated with

80

tar. They had one mast with a large square sail, and on the side, there were places for oars, but even the oars looked too feeble for their purpose. Men were waiting by the boats each holding an oar upright at his side. Oswald reckoned they were not quite twice the height of a man in their length.

Never before had Oswald noticed any clear expression of fear on Cedric's face, but there was today as he stared at these boats. So much so, that Oswald was distracted from his own apprehension.

Eanfrith, Oswiu and Oswald would travel together with some of Queen Acha's household; the boat would leave *them* on Iona and take the *rest* on to the island of Coll with his mother.

King Eochaid Buide, his children and some warriors, one of whom was Daffyd, had come with them to see them on their way. Cedric had quite taken to the warrior; he was even now talking and *laughing* with him, as if they had been friends for years. No doubt, Cedric was seeking confirmation from him that these craft were indeed seaworthy.

Meanwhile the men from the boats were carefully stowing their belongings on the little craft, under the supervision of Torem.

'I wish I were coming with you, Prince Oswald,' Helen said looking genuinely sorry that she was going to be left behind.

'Awe, that is kind of you Princess,' and Oswald hugged her. 'Sadly they do not allow women on the island.'

'Do you think that is fair?'

'Well... I don't know,' he said facing her, his hands resting on her shoulders and looking sympathetically into her eyes.

'I'm going to marry you, Prince Oswald of Bernicia...' she unexpectedly blurted out.

Oswald eyes widened, with total incredulity. At the great age of twelve, marriage was not at the forefront of his thoughts this day. Her face froze, embarrassed that she had bared her heart to him. She had even surprised herself and now felt foolish; *he* clearly did not feel the same. Oswald saw her eyes fill with tears; she was about to cry.

'If I was to have you for a wife, I should think myself very fortunate indeed, you honour me, if it is your wish then it is mine too,' he quickly added, and her tears slowly turned to smiles, as if the sun had unexpectedly appeared from behind a cloud heralding a summer's day. She kissed him on his cheek and hugged him once more. Oswald slowly released his hold on the princess, and went to where his mother and friends from Bernicia were gathered. He embraced Hrodulf and Cedric and thanked them both, certain that they would care for his mother.

'Please don't say anything to my mother about our recent conversation, I don't want to hurt her,' he whispered to Cedric as he held him. Cedric responded by briefly tightening his grip signifying that he understood. Finally, Oswald held his mother who was unable to prevent her tears.

'I will miss you son, do take care of young Oswiu, he is so young to be on his own, and I'm fond of him.'

'I will Mother, and he will not be on his own, I will be with him. You know how close we are, you can reassure his mother. I have told her not to worry and promised to care for him.'

She kissed him and held him, reluctant to let him go.

'Thank you son, you have always been a good boy and I have forever loved you as my own, have I not?'

So, what Cedric had told him was now confirmed, was that what she had meant, be it unintentionally?

'Yes, I could ask no more from any mother,' and with those parting words he kissed her once more, prised himself free of her, and walked into the water to the curragh.

With a little help, Oswald clambered gingerly over the side of the boat, fearing that he might put his foot through the rather flimsy looking skin. He felt the structure flex even as he took his place on the wooden thwart. [16] The curragh rose and fell most unsettlingly as the waves rolled up onto the white sandy beach.

In many ways, this was not unlike the beach at Bebbanburg. He'd always thought that the coast and beaches of his home were the finest and could not be bettered, but he had to concede, that this beach, though smaller, was almost the equal of the beautiful long stretches of golden sand between the sea and the fort of Bebbanburg.

Suddenly there was a violent jerked as the little boat was pushed free from the grip of the sand, Oswald was caught off-guard, and almost tumbled back over from his seat. At the command, "PULL", the oars fought as one to overcome the momentum of the incoming swell. *Gradually* – with a final fused dip of the paddles, they were rewarded with their freedom, and the little craft glided across the water like a bird floating on a breath of air, and into their future.

Oswald became quickly aware of the ingenuity of this ever-flexing marvel. He could see how it in fact twisted and bowed in perfect harmony with the rise and fall of the swell, as if it had a living rapport with the ocean. He actually felt much safer on this little boat than he had when he'd travelled on bigger boats with his father, Æthelfrith, to the islands off the coast of Bebbanburg. Alas, as he glanced at Eanfrith, *his* face told a different story.

As the large square sail was being unfurled, it rebelled for a moment then billowed contentedly as it surrendered its will to the unrelenting persuasion of the wind.

Oswald turned to look back at the shore, which was now disappearing surprisingly quickly into the distance. Already those left behind were turning from people into merely unrecognisable shapes, but he could yet see one small arm waving, and responded likewise until he could see it no longer.

He had been told that they would not reach Iona until the evening; it was about fourteen leagues travel. They had first to negotiate between two islands off the mainland before they were on the open sea. Oswald thanked the sea gods that they were at peace this day. Calm as it was, his head felt a little unsteady, as did his gut.

He hoped too that his mother and Cedric would be safe. Their intention, he'd been told, was to beach and make camp for the night on the island of Muile, [17] continuing on their journey next day. They would have another half day's sailing to the island of Coll. It would be unnecessarily dangerous to travel through the night and it was pointless to take such risk. Oswald wished that Cedric had come with *him* and stayed the night on Iona before they went on, but women were forbidden on the island and he would not leave Queen Acha. Oswald though that was true, but he suspected that Cedric didn't want to be anywhere near the monk priests, and was only too happy to have his *duty* as an excuse for forgoing that option.

There was shouting and waving of farewells as the boats separated. Acha might not be his birth mother, but she was the only mother he'd ever known, and he knew this would be no small thing to her. Oswald watched her sitting quietly at the rear of the craft; Cedric was standing next to her. Oswald stared for some time even after the boats, with all he knew, disappeared into the haze. It was quiet now; all he could hear was the gentle ripple of the sea as the boat sliced its way through the water and the occasional flap of the sail, fleetingly luffing as it lost the wind.

The warriors on Oswald's craft would be taken on to Coll after the three princes had been delivered to their new home.

It was yet light when the island came into view – they had made good time. Oswald was mesmerised by the crystal clear water, he could almost see down to the seabed. They were cutting through shoals of tiny fish, which swam off in every direction.

Ahead of them was the rocky coastline of Iona. The curragh, adjusted its final tack making towards a small sandy inlet, ideally suited for beaching their craft safely.

Set back from the shoreline, he could see what he supposed was to be their new home. It consisted of a small group of stone buildings; one was much larger than the rest, Oswald guessed that it was the temple of their gods. He assumed that they had chosen stone to build with instead of wood, because of the lack of trees. He could not see a single tree on the island, but there was stone aplenty.

As they neared the beach, two men quickly rose from their places, and in a well practised manoeuvre, took in the sail, neatly wrapping and binding it to the crossbeam, and the small craft glided gently up the sand, then nestled peacefully onto its side.

Two other men leapt over the bow of the boat with ropes, and skilfully tied the boat to posts dug into the ground, no doubt for that very purpose.

The headman ordered them to disembark and make their way up to the "Monastery" as they called it, saying his men would see that their baggage was carried there for them.

Eanfrith look strangely subdued, not his normal ebullient self, but then Oswald knew what Eanfrith was like; he was never confident when he was amongst strangers. He felt sorry for him at this moment. As Cedric had once said; anyone with the constant need to be assertive; was not a secure person. Oswald knew that for now *he* would have to take the lead *without* making Eanfrith feel threatened, but he was used to doing that, so it would be no hardship.

This holy place was obviously yet in a state of ongoing construction even after sixty years. There were buildings that he supposed were where the priest monks lived.

They were taken to the larger of the dwellings. Oswald saw one of the priest monks, an elderly shabbily dressed man with short unkempt hair, and a big cross on his chest, with an equally big smile on his face. He was standing at the door to welcome them, surprisingly, in their own native tongue.

'Welcome, welcome, young Princes, come inside and we will find mete for you. I am the Abbot Fergno,' he said and he bowed humbly to them.

The hall was poorly lit; it took a moment for their eyes to adjust to the gloom. Oswald could see that it was a clean but drab place totally lacking in colour.

'Be seated,' said the Abbot smiling

Eanfrith was quiet, as was Oswald, for he suddenly felt to be a long way from Bebbanburg, Oswiu pressed closely to Oswald and Oswald put his arm around him.

The three took the places offered at the long table and the Abbot sat down opposite them.

Young men in plain, coarse, woven, drab robes, which were perfectly suited to their surroundings, came with wooden bowls and platters, filled with fish, beans and small loaves of fresh bread. It was plain fare, but welcome mete for they had eaten little since they'd left Dunadd that morning. There was drink too, a strange sweet drink, the Abbot said was called mead, and was made from honey. He told the princes that they kept honeybees here on the island; and caring for the bees was one of the many skills the young monks learned, as part of their devotions to God.

'We believe that one's whole life should be an offering to God. He is interested about every little thing we do, therefore we should do *everything* as if we were doing it just for Him.'

Oswald thought the Abbot's god was easily pleased, if keeping bees was a devotion to him. Everyone knew that it was great deeds of valour, which pleased their Saxon gods, not, humble bee keeping. No wonder the followers of this Christian god were always being killed by the Saxons.

The Abbot went on to tell them that they tried to make and grow all they needed, here on the island. Their greatest need was timber for their building work. Oswald had already noticed there were no trees on the island, or none to speak of, so of course all their timber would have to be ferried from the mainland.

'Tell me first, what are we to call you handsome young men? I was given a note of the names of those who were coming, but I do not know, to which face, to affix which name. I love to know people's names,' he said smiling at each of them. 'Names are so important; they denote us as unique individuals, a *single* word which identifies us, and to some extent defines us. What a special thing. For example, one of you is called Oswald, so I'm informed,' he looked at each enquiringly and smiled. '"Os", means god, and "Wald", comes from the Saxon word, "Weald" which means, *rules*. Therefore, "Oswald" means *God Rules*. A fine name that is a statement every time it is spoken, perhaps you do not share my amusement?' he said smiling once more.

They all stared at this strange man. 'I am Oswald,' Oswald said feeling proud that it was his name, 'this is Prince Eanfrith, now the Lord of Bebbanburg, and the youngest of us is Prince Oswiu,' he said placing a comforting arm round Oswiu.

'I am honoured to meet you all. You are here to study and learn so I'm told.'

'Our god is Wōden, not your half eaten god. We do not eat *our* gods,' Eanfrith asserted with all the bravado he could muster.

The Abbot turned to him and smiled, nothing seemed to fluster this man. He was most annoyingly serene.

'You are a devout man, I take it Lord?'

'What do you mean, devout?'

'Simply that you follow your god with commitment and sincerity.'

Eanfrith looked flustered, 'we have *many* gods. You only have three gods, and you eat them. You see, I know all there is to know about your gods.'

'Ah, you are clearly a very clever young man for I am still learning, but I am old and slow to learn, you will need to be patient with me I'm afraid. I will be interested to hear about all these gods of yours. I am always eager to learn, it helps me to understand, and understanding helps me govern wisely. I hope in time to share with you what *I* have learned and that you will share with me what *you* have learned, and we will walk together on this great journey of life by learning from each other.'

'What shall we call you Lord?' asked Oswald hoping to divert Eanfrith, for it was clear that this old man was far cleverer than Eanfrith, and Eanfrith was in danger of making himself look like a fool.

'I am referred to as Father, because we are a family here and I am the head, the Father of our family, metaphorically speaking. I hope you will feel as if you are *part* of our small community, certainly, as long as you are here, we will endeavour to treat you as such. You are free to come to me at any time if you are concerned in any way or even if you merely wish to talk. I love to talk, my weakness I'm afraid,' he lifted his hands, and, shrugged his shoulders at the confession of his shortcoming.

'How long will we be here – Father?' asked Oswald adjusting his seating position.

'Ah...' the Abbot smile, at Oswald's awkwardness, 'now that is a difficult question, when you have learned enough, shall we say,' he offered ambiguously. 'Does that answer your question?'

Eanfrith's frustration manifested itself by him banging his fist on the table causing the plates to leap in the air. The Abbot never flinched, but both Oswald and Oswiu jumped in time with the platters.

'I am now twenty-one and a man, a King... I know all I need to know.'

The Abbot bowed his head respectfully, 'I am honoured that you are amongst us, Lord, no doubt I can learn much from you, perhaps you will help me with my knowledge of Saxon ways. I speak a little of your tongue, but I am ignorant of so much about your people. If I am to be a friend of your people a greater knowledge of them and their ways can only help me, to that end we are indeed honoured and privileged that you are here.'

'Where are we to sleep, Father?' Oswald once again stepped in quickly, before Eanfrith had a chance to further shame himself by his hostile behaviour.

'I will leave you now, but when you have eaten, Brother Aidan will show you the rooms we have prepared for you.' One of the young men who had brought the food to them who was standing behind the Abbot, bowed. Oswald thought this monk was slightly older than himself, perhaps seventeen. Oswald smiled congenially at him. 'Because of your seniority, Lord Eanfrith, you will have a room to yourself and you two young Lords, will share a room. We thought that Lord Oswiu might benefit from the comfort of your company, Lord Oswald. You will be in a hall where there are other young men, who are studying to become full members of our community. Their wish is to devote their lives to God.'

'Your god,' Eanfrith asserted.

'Yes, forgive me, I refer to my God.'

'Thank you Father, that is kind,' Oswald said speedily, Eanfrith did no more than give a brief grunt. It was clear to Oswald that this man was not easily provoked, and was equal to the hostility Eanfrith was exhibiting.

The three princes ate in silence. While they ate, the monk named Aidan, stood with his back to the wall and never uttered a word. The silence in this place was so insidious that Oswald felt overwhelmed by it. He kept thinking about his name, "God Rules", it made him tremble at the thought, how was he to understand such a thing, what did it mean? Suddenly, he wanted to shout out – to bring some release from the deafening noise in his head, – *but* – he did no more than smile at Oswiu. He wondered if his brothers were feeling the same as he. He glanced at Eanfrith, but he seemed only concerned with the mete before him. Oswald remembered Helen saying to him that he *thought* too much, perhaps he did.

Once they'd finished the meal, Aidan, with a graceful sweep of his hand, indicated that they were to follow him. He took them to a small dwelling with two floors. There were stone steps leading up to the second floor at one end, which overlooked the space below where there were several sleeping places laid out for the night. Oswald assumed, as he looked down, that they must be for the other young people, who the Abbot had mentioned. He thought that they probably cleared away the space in the morning.

They were indeed to be privileged with their own individual rooms. The rooms were basic without adornment, each enclosed with a rough looking door. The boards on the doors had wide gaps between them; they had obviously dried out and shrunk since the doors were first made. The walls were plain white limewashed and the only decoration was a cross, painted on the wall. There was none of the brightly painted decoration depicting animals and elaborate patterns on the walls with which he was familiar. Oswald guessed the cloth bags that were to be their beds were packed with hay or perhaps even wool. He'd seen that there were many sheep on the island, and there were drab wool rugs to cover them if they were cold; the same as they'd seen laid out downstairs.

Oswiu lay down on his bed and smiled for the first time. 'This is really quite comfortable Oswald, and it's warm too.'

'I hope that Eanfrith feels as you do,' Oswald whispered, hoping that his voice didn't carry to the next room. He knew that Eanfrith had a wooden frame bed at Bebbanburg; he didn't lie on the floor like a servant.

'Are you missing your mother, Oswald?' Oswiu asked sadly, his smile having been no more than a fleeting expression of comfort.

'A little, but we have each other and I was told that I would see her often; I will remember that promise when I think of her. It has been a *long* journey from Bernicia has it not, I think about our people there. I hope that King Edwin treats them kindly. Together, we will make the most of what we have here, daily supporting, and encouraging each other. Agreed?'

'I will do my best Oswald, but I feel lonely, I wish my mother was here with us. I know she will be missing me too. She gave me this little bag filled with lavender,' Oswiu held the small bag up for Oswald to see, 'she said I must remember her when I smelt it. She always smells of lavender, doesn't she.'

'That's true, but you know her better than me. She will be with you every moment in her thoughts, I'm sure of it, and you will see her when we go back to Dunadd.'

Oswald unwrapped his belongings and amongst them was his prized sword.

'You have brought your new sword, I didn't know that, do you think you will need it here?'

97

'I know not, but this sword is more precious to me than you can ever imagine, it will never leave my side as long as I live.'

Chapter 9

Death of a Queen

Over the last year, Oswald had been to see his mother several times because she was ill. He was ever more worried about her deteriorating health, which she could no longer pretend was as it should be. He knew she was unwell and had been since they'd travelled from Bernicia, perhaps even before that and he'd found it particularly distressing on this visit, to see the marked deterioration in her health.

He was quiet as they sailed home to Iona, and leant back against the side of the curragh with his head hung between his legs in despair. When they beached he leapt wearily from the boat without a word, paused for a moment and made his way at some pace up to the monastery.

Brother Aidan had to walk quickly to catch up to him. 'You have been very quiet on the journey home,' Brother Aidan panted as he spoke. He was usually a man of few words, so Oswald knew these were words spoken with kind intent.

Oswald slowed his pace, looked into Aidan's eyes, and spoke in a soft tired voice. 'Forgive me if I have given offence my friend, it was not my intention. I'm concerned about Mother, no doubt you realise that. Each time I leave I wonder if it will be the last time I will see her, and that is so hard, I can't do anything, you see.'

'I know... it is the hardest thing when we see those we love suffering. We might not *always* understand another's anguish, but we all have mother's whom we love and losing one's mother is a very painful thing. You are my dear friend too, so believe me, I care how you feel.'

'Thank you Aidan, you are always understanding. Yes, it's true, our mother's are indeed special, but you have never mentioned your family, and I have never thought to ask. I'm ashamed that our conversations have always been about my concerns.'

'I never saw it like that, Lord. My life is not about me, my friend; it is about my Saviour, who made Himself known to me when I was a small boy in Hibernia. I was only perhaps – seven or eight. Since that day, He has consumed my life, and in that – I have – *found* – life, in such abundance I could never have imagined that it was possible.'

'You are a very special man, Aidan, and I believe the gods have bound you and I together in some way for a reason.'

Aidan didn't reply, he merely smiled, touched Oswald's shoulder and they walked on without further comment. At the door of the building where they slept, Oswald paused and stroked his chin thoughtfully.

'You go on Aidan, I will join you shortly.' Aidan dipped his head and went in. Oswald stood for a moment longer, as if unsure what to do, turned and walked to where he hoped that he might find Brother Ségéne. He went into the building and asked a monk if he'd seen Brother Ségéne, the monk nodded in the direction of the Brother's cell. Brother Ségéne, was one of the most senior monks and had his own place of work where he also slept, which they called cells.

Oswald knocked and a voice bade him enter.

'Brother Ségéne.'

'Ah, Prince Oswald, come on in, you've been very much in my thoughts, so you have,' Brother Ségéne said rising from his chair. 'Be seated – how can I help?'

'As you know, I have been to see my mother.'

'Yes, the Abbot told me where you were. I gave Brother Aidan some mead for her, the honey in it has healing properties, and it may bring her some relief, it will do no harm. How was the Queen?'

'Thank you, he did give it to her – She is ill, as you know. I fear she is going to die, her skin was an awful shade of yellow and she is so thin, her eyes were as white as white could be. They have tried all manner of things, but nothing seems to make any difference.'

'That is sad. I met the Queen once, when I went to preach on Coll; she was a very gentle, gracious lady. I'm very sorry, Oswald. You could have stayed if you had wished.'

'I know, I know, in truth – it was difficult to leave her, but she has old friends around her and my brothers. I was worried about Oswiu; here on his own, he needs my company.'

'It's true, how was he when you returned, I have been keeping an eye on him, but sure enough he misses you?'

'I have not yet seen him; I came first to see you Brother. I think Brother Aidan will go to him, Oswiu likes him.'

'I have noticed, Brother Aidan is a good soul and has a kind heart. I pray daily for your mother my friend, as I do for you all.'

'It seems *your* god is not any better at answering our requests than mine is.'

'So it might appear. I agree that it is difficult to believe in any being, real or imagined, if that being does not touch our lives here and now when we have needs. We all want to ease the hurts of the people we love. That is the hardest part of loving, suffering with them. Caring so much we would give our own lives for them, if we could. This is the measure of real love, putting others before our own wants.'

'Brother Aidan has just this moment said the same thing to me.'

'Yes, he would, he has a rare love for God. I believe that the only thing that God asks of *us* is to believe that He loves us – just as we are, because we can never be as we should be. Isn't that what we all need to hear sometimes, from those we love, that they love us unconditionally. Forgiveness is at the heart of my God. As I have told you before the central message at the beating heart of the Christian faith, is about a *relationship* between the Creator and the created: my Creator and me, and my God wants such a relationship with everyone, no matter how lowly and unworthy one is or feels. From what you tell me, your gods only have time for those who succeed, the great warriors, not those who struggle in this life.'

'I don't seem to know anything anymore, but, we all want to feel well and happy and we will follow the one who we think can best achieve this. Perhaps *your* god is the *only* god, I know not the truth of it. I do know that *you* are different, different from anyone I have ever known.'

'Is that a commendation or a criticism, my friend?' Ségéne laughed. 'Let me share some good news, your brother Eanfrith has accepted our Christian faith and was baptised while you have been away.'

'Eanfrith!'

'Yes, he has not progressed with his studies as *you* have; perhaps he was too old when he came. He wished to return to Dunadd as a Christian. You look surprised, Oswald.'

'I am, he has never shown any great understanding, or interest in your faith.'

'Mmm, in truth, just how sincere his commitment is, I do not know, but it is not for me to judge another. Time will tell; God is not fooled by man. I will pray for him.'

'When will he leave?'

'He has already gone, a curragh towing barges with timber for the ongoing work landed and he returned to the mainland with them.'

'I don't know what to say,' Oswald could do no more than shake his head slowly from side to side.

'Then say nothing my friend. Go and see Oswiu, perhaps we will talk more on the morrow when you have slept.'

Oswald stared at Brother Ségéne for a moment, turned, reached for the door handle and left without further comment.

Oswald wearily climbed the stone steps to his room, the door was open and he saw Aidan sitting next to Oswiu on his bed.

'*Oswald,*' Oswiu, leaped from his bed and jumped into Oswald's arms. 'You're home, I'm so pleased to see you.'

'Come, sit down.'

'Has Brother Aidan made known to you of our time away?'

'Yes, I'm sorry to hear about your mother, Oswald.'

'Thank you; tell me what do you know of Eanfrith?'

'He has become one of the Christians and returned to the fort at Dunadd.'

'So I have been told by Brother Ségéne; I went to see him before I came here to you. Thank you Brother Aidan, I'll stay with Oswiu. We have much to talk about, you must be tired too,' Oswald said, turning his attention to Aidan.

'Thank you Prince Oswald, but I will go to Abbot Fergno first before I make for my bed, he will want to know how the Queen is keeping, as I see it.'

Oswald stood and embraced Aidan then sat down again beside his brother as Aidan left. He told him about his fears for his mother's health. Changing the subject once more, he asked Oswiu what, if anything,

Eanfrith had said to him. Oswiu told him, that Eanfrith had said that he now believed in the Christian God and was going to be baptised and then he would return to Dunadd as soon as it was possible. He returned two days past when a trader landed on the island.

'Mmm, it seems sudden; he never mentioned anything about his thoughts to me. He always seemed to be antagonistic towards the Christian God.'

'Yes, I was as surprised as you are.'

As the time passed, Oswald was becoming ever more fluent with his new language of Hibernian, and of course, it was Ségéne's native tongue, so he was delighted with Oswald's progress. The studying was not a problem, Oswald actually enjoyed the work, as did Oswiu, and they would engage in discussions about their studies even in their spare time.

Eventually the inevitable word came to him via Brother Ségéne, his mentor who'd become more like a friend – Queen Acha had died. Oswald found it difficult when his mentor explained that he and Oswiu would have to attend the burial without any of his new friends from Iona, because the Christian monks could not be part of the pagan ritual.

The preparations for Oswald and Oswiu were made quickly and as they stood before the boat, Brother Aidan pushed a small piece of polished stone, in the shape of a fish, into Oswald's hand. He explained that he had found it on the beach on a day when he had been wrestling with a particular thought about God, and since then he had always carried it in his pocket. 'Holding it in my hand reminds me of my creator and that he works all things together for good for those who love him. I want you to know that though we have been forbidden by the Abbot to go with you in body, I will be with you in spirit.' Oswald smiled at the kindness of this gentle monk and put the stone in his pocket.

For the first time Oswald was conscious of an internal challenge to his thoughts and beliefs. He couldn't talk to Oswiu at this moment, his thoughts were too muddled to tell them to someone else, he could only stare at the rolling sea as they sailed steadily on towards the island of Coll. Strangely it was as peaceful as the monastery out here this day. All that could be heard, as Oswald stood holding the main shroud, was the odd cry of a lone seagull and the creaking of the mast and rigging as they moved leisurely in harmony with the wind and the waves,

His hand felt the stone in his pocket. There was so much about this Christian faith, which seemed to make sense, and more and more of his long held pagan beliefs, which did *not* make sense anymore. Somehow, the Christian God seemed so much bigger, even bigger than Wōden. *His* beliefs had always been based around fate, the whim of the gods, what would be would be; it was simply down to fate when this, or that happened. The Christian faith, as far as he could understand it, was about a relationship between man and this God. Man had been separated from the Christian God because of his "Sin". Sin, that's what they called it, it wasn't a word that he'd really thought about before or understood. It seemed to mean that we were not living our lives as was intended, and falling short of the best God had for man. Apparently, man had chosen to reject God in favour of his own way and this "Jesus" had come to restore that broken relationship and *would* – do so if we would only let Him. Oswald couldn't quite understand the need for Him to die, however this man came and was tortured to death. If nothing else, Oswald could understand by this action, how much mankind had meant to Him. Now mankind had once again access to this living God, *because* of this Jesus' death on a cross.

'OSWALD!' Oswiu shouted.

'Sorry Oswiu, did you want something? I was thinking,' and as soon as the words left his lips he had to smile – for he could hear Princess Helen's voice teasing him, saying that he thought too much.

'Here, have something to eat,' Oswiu passed him some bread and goat's cheese.

'Ah, thank you, Oswiu, what would I do without you?' Oswald smiled at him as he bit into the cheese.

Chapter 10

New Life

It was good to see Cedric and Hrodulf standing on the shore to welcome them, even though the purpose of this visit was one Oswald did not relish.

'I've missed you my two young Princes,' Cedric said sadly, wrapping them both in

111

his arms. Whilst Cedric held them, Hrodulf laid his hands on their heads and greeted them with his blessing.

The funeral rite would be tomorrow, Cedric informed Oswald as they made their way to the village. A tomb had been prepared, and a wooden room had been built where all that was necessary for the afterlife would be placed, such as food and drink for the journey and some of her most precious personal items of jewellery and trinkets as was befitting the great queen she was.

The next day Queen Acha was laid inside the room and it was sealed, and finally it would all be covered with soil and turf to form a protective mound.

As Oswald stood with Hrodulf and Cedric, watching the closing of his mother's tomb, Cedric leaned close to him and said, 'Your mother commissioned me to tell you the story of your birth mother. I made no mention to her about your father being Lord Wulfstan. She always thought that your father was her husband King Æthelfrith. I told your mother not to worry, that I'd already made everything known to you. At first, she was surprised, and then she was pleased that you had never treated her any differently, in spite of your knowledge. She said to tell you how much she loved you, that you could not have been more precious – had you been her own.'

Oswald's head bowed and he felt the tears, which had until that moment been held on the edge of his eyelid, gradually overflow and trickle down his cheek. He was glad that she was at peace after all her suffering over the last years, and he asked the Christian God – if He would recognize that she had done her best, and that He would forgive her pagan beliefs, and his too, she was innocent, a lady without guile.

At that instant, it came like a bolt of lightning from the heavens, it struck him so forcefully that he actually staggered and nearly fell. Cedric instinctively reached for his arm, assuming he had been overcome with grief, but it was not grief, it was the complete opposite to grief. He was engulfed in what seemed like a cloud of love. He *knew* at that second, that the Christian God was real. He didn't know why, or how, or what had happened, but he knew that something irreversible had taken place and his life would never be the same again.

Cedric kept asking him if he was all right, he even shook him slightly, but he couldn't tell Cedric, not at this moment, he would never understand, but he *hoped* that Oswiu would. He could see so clearly now that the grave goods would not provide for his mother's afterlife, that was man limiting God to his understanding. Their human offering merely affixed what was of this life – to this life, and in the end, they would all be swallowed up by the ground, as would the *earthly* body of his mother.

He understood that this hope he now felt was beyond the physical world of touch and feel, that in him was living a new creation, which was eternal and would not perish; *he* was *more* than that which walked and breathed this day's air. He couldn't understand it, perhaps he never would, but he was certain that he had been touched by the living God, as certain as night followed day.

There was a burning feeling inside, his face felt flushed, strength seemed to be flowing into his arms right down to his finger tips, he flexed his hands. He was alive like never before, as if his life was suddenly filled with the brightest colours. He wanted to shout it to all who were standing there. "GOD RULES", that was actually his own name, God would rule in *his* life from now on, he swore it. He would not be defined by his title, or parentage, how his life had played out, or the things that had, or *would* happen to him, *he* would be defined by who he was in the Christ God.

On the way back to the village, Oswald asked Cedric what he would do now that the queen was dead. He said that he would stay here until *he* and Oswiu had finished their time on Iona then he would return to Dunadd with them.

'Did you know Eanfrith is to marry one of King Eochaid Buide's daughters, Princess Edlin?'

'No, you are better informed than I am, Cedric. I don't recall this daughter, *Edlin* did you say? I never heard Princess Helen mention such a sister.'

'Edlin, I'm sure it was. Do you remember the name Hrodulf?'

'As far as I remember it was as you say.'

Oswald shrugged his shoulders, 'it's all news to me.'

'I imagine we get more traders here than on your island, there are more people here to trade with.'

'When is this marriage to take place?'

'I know not, but I imagine that we will be sent for, they will want Bernicia to have as many of her people there as possible, few as we are. I thought that Eanfrith might have come here today, and he could have told us for himself.'

'I wondered if he would come, did you send word to him?'

'Yes, he knew, right enough.'

'Will Hrodulf stay here too?'

'Aye, we have nowhere else to go and we are both getting older,' he smiled. 'We will farm and fish, it's not a bad life, we'll take turns at being the king,' he smiled again, 'but as I have said, we will be there for you when the time comes, never fear.'

Oswald wondered what he meant by, "When the *time* comes", but he didn't pursue it. It began to rain as they walked back; stirred up by the westerly wind off the sea, it was bitterly cold and the rain cut into Oswald's face like shards of ice.

They began to run, 'Quick lad, let's get into the hall and drink some of the Celtic *water of life*, before we catch a dose of the ague. It will melt the ice in your veins, aye, and dry the wool on your back too.' Cedric laughed as they entered the rather dark dank hall. It was like the barrow they'd only just left and a shiver ran through Oswald at the thought of his dear mother all alone.

Oswald put his nose to the earthenware cup Cedric had passed into his hand, the

116

fumes made his eyes water. He nervously sipped it and gasped, it took his breath away. Cedric was right, whatever was in this pale yellow water, it either warmed you, or numbed your senses, so you simply forgot that you were cold in the first place. Oswald wasn't sure which it was.

Oswiu couldn't get to his feet to wave farewell he'd been carried to the awaiting curragh. He was now lying awkwardly on some curled up rope as they were pushed away from the small jetty, and the men began to unfurl the sail. He looked as if death would be a mercy to him and Oswald was feeling only marginally better. A night of drinking the Celtic water of life, or uisge beatha as they called it – to celebrate the journey of Queen Acha to the afterlife, seemed to be bringing anything *but* life to the pair and Oswiu only had one cup of the elixir the whole night. Oswald had only a little more than Oswiu and still he didn't know how he could possibly survive until they reached Iona, so ill did he feel, and he slumped down next to his brother and closed his eyes.

Chapter 11

Return to Dunadd

It was mid-afternoon before they arrived home at Iona.

It appeared that while they'd been away, Abbot Fergno had also been informed of the forthcoming marriage. He'd been sent word that Eanfrith was to marry, and Oswald and Oswiu had been instructed to attend by Queen Bebba, as part of the royal Bernician family. Oswald couldn't take in the information at this moment, so thick was his head, he needed to sleep, but he knew he would look forward to going once he had recovered.

He wondered if Helen was yet convinced that she would marry him, and he managed a token smile at the thought. She'd probably forgotten him by now; young girls were ever imagining they were in love and thinking about marrying. He thought that she might not recognise him with his new beard, thin as it was, he was proud of it.

As they approached the village of An Crìonan, [18] where they would leave their curragh and walk the short distance to the fort of Dunadd, Oswald could see the people waiting for them. He hoped one of those hands waving would be the hand of Princess Helen.

His eyes burned as they scanned the faces through the evening haze, *yes*, she was there. His heart leapt as he saw her smiling. He knew that it was foolishness, they had only known each other for no more than a week, but she was there and smiling, that was enough for his heart. He was fifteen now, she would be fourteen.

Queen Bebba was there too and already Oswiu was calling to her, it had been several months since he'd seen her. He'd always used his free time to visit Dunadd whenever Oswald had gone to visit his mother on Coll, but it had still been difficult for him.

The boat settled in the same spot where it had sailed from all that time since. Even the sharp stab of pain, as he looked to the spot where he'd hugged his mother before they'd set off that day, did not tarnish the excitement of their arrival. Oswald playfully pushed Oswiu and jumped from the side before him, splashing, up to his knees in the cold water. Oswiu jumped next to him and was pleased to see that he'd drenched Oswald, but it didn't matter, nothing could spoil this day.

'Mother...' was all Oswiu could say. She was standing with his sister Æbbe who seemed every bit as excited as Oswiu as he ran into their arms.

Helen and Oswald briefly hesitated now that they were in touching distance of each other, but for no more than a moment and then they too embraced, she even kissed him.

'Oswald, you can't know how happy I am. This moment has been in my every thought ever since I knew that you were coming to Edlin's wedding and before if I'm being honest. Are you happy too?'

'What do you think? Look you are all wet now because of me, I'm sorry, I will get my own back on Oswiu for this,' he laughed.

'I don't care how wet I am, it took me all my time not to swim out to meet you,' and she kissed him once more. 'Your face looks different...' she rocked her head slowly from one side to the other as she looked at him.

'Do you like it,' he said proudly.

'It's wonderful you are a man now,' that was the perfect answer to a young warrior. 'Come let's walk on ahead so we can talk, you can tell me all your thoughts, or have you ceased all your thinking?' she teased and they both laughed.

'Before we rush off I must speak to the Queen.' Oswald turned to Queen Bebba. 'My Lady, it is good to see you looking so well,' he said bowing.

'Oswald... it is good to see you, you have grown into a man since we last met.'

'I have missed you too, *Swald*,' Æbbe said jumping in to her mother's welcome, and he smiled at her use of his pet name.

'You've grown, my favourite pest,' he said laughing and wrapping her in his arms. 'But I will leave you for a short while, I am going to walk ahead with the Princess, we will talk later,' and he smiled once more.

'I have much to tell you Helen,' he said to her in her own native Hibernian.

'*Ohh,* very good, you surprise me. Your Hibernian is better than my Saxon.'

'Nonsense you speak very good Saxon. My other news is that I have become a Christian.'

'*Really!*'

'Yes *really*, I have been a Christian for over two months. I have actually been baptized, not once, but twice now, thanks to Oswiu,' and they laughed once more.

'I was sorry to hear that your mother died Oswald. I so wanted to be there for you, but father said it was not my place to go, it was very sad. I have some memories of my own mother dying, but not so many. Most of all I remember how frightened I was. I thought that's what people you loved did; they died and left you. I was afraid to even like anyone for a long time. I want you to know that you can tell me how you feel, *if* you wish, it really matters to me, I want to share everything with you.' Oswald didn't answer her, but he squeezed her hand for he knew she was sincere.

'Did you know Cedric and Hrodulf are here?'

'Thank the Lord, I hoped for that. I wonder why they did not come to the shore to meet me?'

'That is my fault, I'm sorry. I told him how much I love you, and Cedric said he would not take the moment of your arrival from me, that he'd wait at the fort to welcome you. He is the most kind, and beautiful of men, no wonder you love him,'

With that news, Oswald took Helen's hand and they laughed as they ran towards the fort.

Oswald saw Cedric at the gate with a big smile on his face and outstretched welcoming arms. Hrodulf was by his side and Oswald ran into them wrapping them in his arms.

'You get bigger every time we meet Lord, you're almost as tall as me now,' said Hrodulf.

Eanfrith had not gone to the shore to welcome Oswald, but now walked towards them.

'Do you not have a greeting for me, your King, brother?'

Oswald released Cedric and Hrodulf and bowed to Eanfrith, who nodded his approval.

'You look well, I have heard that you have become a Christian, Eanfrith.'

'Yes,' he shrugged his shoulders, 'All gods are much the same, are they not?'

'No, not in the case of the Christian God, He is like no other.' Eanfrith narrowed his eyes warily, and looked suspiciously at Oswald, but said no more. 'I have become a Christian too,' Oswald said glancing at Cedric, whose smile left his face on hearing Oswald's confession.

'I see that you yet have my sword, at your side,' Eanfrith now cast an eye in Cedric's direction, but said no more. Oswald did not respond. Eanfrith would never have this sword, that his father had called "Dream World".

'Walk with me, I will introduce you to your new sister to be, this will be the binding of our two great houses. It will make me stronger when we return to take Bernicia from the usurper, *your* uncle. She is the daughter of King Conadd Cerr, who rules jointly with King Eochaid Buide, I don't think you have ever met him. The two kings are close kin.'

Oswald only listened as he followed Eanfrith. He'd understood that Eanfrith's wife to be was the daughter of King Eochaid Buide and wondered why he could not place her, now he understood. Helen held onto his arm without saying a word. Why do you always have to be like this Eanfrith? Oswald thought despairingly.

They walked the short distance into a longhouse and a girl lifted her head and smiled. She looked surprisingly like Helen; this must be Princess Edlin thought Oswald as they neared the girl.

Eanfrith bowed, 'My Lady, this is my brother Prince Oswald. Oswald, this is Princess Edlin.'

'It is an honour to meet you my Lady, this is a very important time for you, you are welcome into our family.'

'Thank you Prince Oswald, I hear that you are a scholar, how kind of you to greet me in my own language,' she cast her eyes at Eanfrith, who had struggled with the work of learning Hibernian and insisted she spoke Saxon.

'I'm sure you will want to find out where you are to stay. I think your friend will help you,' she glanced at Helen and they both smiled.

'I will show the Prince, we will see you at the night's feast, Edlin.'

'Yes, we will talk more then.' With that, Helen took Oswald's hand and led him out of the longhouse.

'She seems nice.'

'She is, we are good friends.'

'How old is she?'

'Seventeen.'

'What do you think of Eanfrith?'

She was hesitant... 'Honestly – I don't like him much, I'm sorry to say this as he is your brother, forgive me.'

'It's all right; I know that he can be difficult to like sometimes. I don't think he likes himself very much. He has always wanted people to respect him, but he is not a bad person. I have learned how to deal with him over the years and we get along tolerably well, as long as he has not to compete with me. I usually let him win, it makes for a better relationship.'

'I will try to like him for your sake and for Edlin. It is their marriage on the morrow and our Priest will give them God's blessing.'

Helen took Oswald to where he was to sleep. She said that she had things to do for Edlin.

'I will see you at the feast,' she kissed Oswald and left him. Her timing was perfect, for Oswald saw Cedric coming towards him, and he knew he would have to face his displeasure.

'*Cedric.*'

'Prince Oswald.'

'I imagine I am facing a storm, because I have become a Christian.'

'No, I understand how difficult it must be for you living with all those priest monks on that island. I would probably have done the same in your position.'

Oswald was at first stunned by Cedric's ready acceptance. Then he realised that Cedric thought that he was merely being pragmatic, to make his life less complicated on Iona.

'Cedric, I think that you have misunderstood.'

'Misunderstood, in what way?'

'I am not merely being practical and doing what would make my life less complicated or that I have collapsed under pressure,' Cedric narrowed his eyes wondering what Oswald was about to say, in his heart not wanting to believe what he feared. 'I have actually given my life to the Christian God.'

It took a moment for Cedric to respond in a calm measured manner. 'You *really* believe in this half eaten god!'

'Yes, I do.'

'But you know fine well that Wōden would gobble up what's left of him in one mouthful. Wōden is the god of gods.'

'I understand what you say Cedric. If you will listen, I will tell you about this God I now follow.' Cedric could only stare, it was clear that he couldn't quite comprehend what Oswald was saying. 'All you have ever taught me is the same as this God says to me. All I could hear from this God's teaching about how to live my life, I have heard from you. Often, I could not understand what you were saying, but now I can, because of this God.'

'You are confusing me Oswald; you have grown too clever with words. You have sorely troubled me son, you know you are everything to me. I would have killed anyone else who talked to me as you have. Ah, it will pass, you have just spent too much time with all this foolishness filling your head,' Cedric said, trying to reassure himself and bring some comfort to the disturbance in his thought world. Oswald understood and chose not to pursue it any further.

Chapter 12

Eanfrith and Edlin

In the evening after they had eaten, Oswald and Helen walked down to the seashore. The night was still with hardly a breath of air. They could hear the revelry they'd left behind them at the fort, floating on the warm night air.

There had been much drinking and feasting, the people were happy. For Oswald all was tinged with sadness, he grieved for his mother, for his home in Bernicia, for his loss of identity, and the uncertainty of his future.

'You are thinking again,' Helen squeezed his hand.

He looked down at her, 'I was thinking how fortunate I am to have someone like you to care for me.'

'Ahh, you were, were you! Does your new found faith permit lies?' she smiled.

'Ha, it's the truth, I am fortunate.'

'But... that is not what you were thinking,' she said shaking her head in disbelief.

'I will have to be careful. Clearly, along with your many talents you have special sight too,' he laughed. 'In truth, I was thinking about all the uncertainty of living, for myself in particular.'

'Oswald Leodwalding of Bernicia, life is simple. When you return from Iona we will be married, have lots of children and live happily ever after, and that's the end of it.'

Oswald laughed, 'of course, whatever was I thinking about, life is that simple, foolish me. Come on, I'll race you to those rocks,' and he pushed her and ran off. When he reached the rocky outcrop, he turned, bent forward with his hands on his knees and panted.

'You cheated, you will never get to heaven,' she called out as she neared and ran into his arms giggling.

'Come on sit down. LOOK, can you see them?' He suddenly blurted out, pointing with his finger.

'What! What are you pointing at? I can't see anything.'

'Dolphins – *look* – several of them, *look* there, can you see them?'

'Oh yes, I see them, how wonderful.'

They were absolutely captivated by the splendour and grace of these beautiful creatures, leaping and diving, in – and – out of the water with barely the slightest disturbance to the surface. They both stood to catch a last glimpse of the display as the dolphins disappeared into the distance.

'I don't remember seeing dolphins so clearly before, Helen.'

'No, a rare sight – I wonder what they were thinking,' she teased and he laughed at her taunt.

'Now there's a thought...'

'Ahhhh, you are impossible, come, we should go back it is getting dark and I must speak with Edlin about the morrow's employment before we sleep, in case there is something she needs me to do.'

'Can I say – how difficult it will be to return to Iona after the wedding? I have so enjoyed the time with you.'

'Don't talk about it, I am absolutely dreading it.' They continued towards the fort in silence for some time.

A grasshopper clicking in the long grass distracted Oswald and suddenly he was aware that there was a competition going on to see who had the loudest click. They stared into the long grass, but neither of them could spot the culprit who'd started the game.

'I pray Helen, that we are not amongst the grasshoppers at Eanfrith's wedding on the morrow, all trying to click louder than the next man. I have found that such gatherings with powerful people present an irresistible opportunity to show that you are better than your enemies and friends.'

'Not just men, women too,' Helen added.

'Aye – women too.'

Oswiu shouted to them as they entered through the gates, he was sitting on a bench with his sister Æbbe. Oswald and Helen sat down beside them.

132

He and Oswiu had never spoken much about their time on Iona, and this was an opportunity to tell Helen and Æbbe of their lives there. To describe the island, explain what they did in their daily studies, all that they'd learned and the interesting people whom they'd met and made friends.

Oswald told them of his weapon practice with his tutor Brother Ségéne, both he and Oswiu smiled at the expression on their faces.

'Brother Ségéne was not always a monk, he was once a warrior of some note and an accomplished swordsman.' He hesitated – then told them of his new faith and all listened intently. Obviously, the undoubted conviction with which he spoke captured their attention, especially Æbbe. Oswald was actually struggling to tell his tale because of her constant interruptions, wanting even more detail.

He could see that Æbbe was mesmerised by his confession.

Helen apologised to them, but said she must go and see Edlin. Oswald also took his leave, as he wanted to see Eanfrith before he settled for the night.

'Please don't go yet Swald, I want you to tell me more.'

'I'm sorry, Æbbe, my beautiful sister, I would like to stay, but I must go. I promise that I will tell you more before I return to Iona.' She was about to argue, but he pointed his finger at her, narrowing his eyes and she resisted her natural inclination to insist, and he smiled and kissed her.

'She loves you, you know.' Helen said quietly as they walked away.

'Ha, I know, and I love her too.'

'But you are an easy man to love, Oswald of Bernicia.'

'You think so do you?'

'I think so.'

Oswald knew that feelings of love and emotions were considered an absurdly flimsy reason for a marriage, which was a match for life. People grew and changed, the binding needed to be something of a more lasting nature. To that end, the two families of Queen Bebba and King Conadd Cerr would have agreed a marriage contract on the betrothal of their children. Even though Eanfrith was not Queen Bebba's son, she was the Queen of his father. The actual marriage ceremony was of less relevance.

Nevertheless, Helen was excited to see them on the morrow; the whole day would be one of spectacle where all would assemble in their finery.

As the couple stood in the midst of their family and friends at the door of their small place of worship, Oswald had to say that Edlin was very beautiful indeed. She wore a white veil of the finest material kept in place on her head by a circlet made of interlaced strands of gold. Her tunic was made of the most beautiful deep blue wool, which signified her purity. It was tied at the waist by a belt, finely plaited from strips of leather with jewels hanging from it. On her breast, she wore two swags of rare coloured glass beads and in the centre of them, a gold and silver brooch set with red garnets.

Eanfrith was equally richly dressed, with a finely woven purple overshirt, Oswald knew that purple was the most expensive of dyes, worn only by kings. It was embroidered on either side of the v shaped neck around the collar, cuffs and at the hem, with rich gold and silver thread. At his waist, he wore a broad leather belt with a magnificent enamel and gold buckle. Attached to it was a bone handled short seax, beautifully inlayed with gold wire, all of which befitted the heir of the royal Bernician King, Æthelfrith.

They exchanged gold rings, which sealed the betrothal contract after which their priest gave his blessing and prayed over them sprinkling holy water upon their heads and anointing them with oil.

In the evening, there was music, dancing and feasting under the stars. Oswald didn't think that he had ever seen Eanfrith look so happy and he was happy for him. Perhaps this would be the making of him and once and for all settle his insecurities.

Whatever Oswald's doubts, he had to say he'd enjoyed the whole occasion, not least the time spent with Helen.

On the morning of their departure, he begged his leave of Helen, saying he must spend some time with his sister Æbbe before he left. Helen understood and reluctantly let him go, she knew that the moment she was dreading was all but upon them.

Oswald found Æbbe sitting by the fort well, she saw him coming and smiled.

'Thank you Swald, I thought that you'd forgotten me and were going without saying goodbye.'

'Now, would I do that to my baby sister, though in truth you are not a baby now.'

'You will always be my Swald. I wanted to talk more to you about your new found faith. You can't know how my heart sang as you shared your story on the day past. The more you talked the more I wanted to hear. You left something burning in me and I wanted to know this Christ God too.'

'It is not a secret for only a few, but it is a gift, free for all. I can't explain it Æbbe, you can tell this God just how you feel and He will answer you, I promise. When I return you can tell me your story, for I know this God will have spoken to you.'

She could only stare at him in disbelief. 'Is that really the truth? But, I must have to do something to please this God!'

'No, believe me, all you need to do is ask, that will please Him more than you can imagine. As I have said, it is His personal gift for you, Æbbe. Come wave goodbye to me then find a quiet place and talk to Him. You can talk to Him at any – time or any – where, but sometimes we have to be in a quiet place to hear Him.'

He took her hand and they walked down to the shore and the awaiting curragh. Helen was already there, she saw him coming and she wiped her face on her sleeve. Oswiu was there with Queen Bebba, as was Cedric and Hrodulf. This was a hellish moment; it could be two years until his return.

He released Æbbe's hand and went to Helen, she tried to smile, but as he tenderly touched her cheek with the back of his hand she burst into tears and clung to him sobbing uncontrollably. Even Cedric was moved to gently lay his gnarled old hand on her shoulder.

'Go Lord, I will take care of the Princess,' she released Oswald and leaned into Cedric's arms. Oswald hesitated for what seemed like forever, turned, and waded into the water. He paused for a moment longer then clambered into the curragh, steadied himself, reached over the side, took Oswiu's hand and helped him onboard.

Once again, there was the familiar sudden jerk as the little craft was freed from the wet sand to begin its wearisome journey back to Iona.

Oswald saw Helen turn her head, but she was unable to wave.

The fort at Bebbanburg 600AD

Chapter 13

Call to Arms

Oswald had adopted some of the monk's ways during his time spent amongst them, it was unavoidable after spending so much time subject to their routines. Now he found as part of his daily life, that he sought out time on his own to reflect on his new faith.

Being born into a royal family had responsibilities and duties that could not be swept aside by personal desires. He owed his allegiance to Bernicia and Eanfirth, but what a joy it would be to be free from these burdens. The monk's practice of solitude and meditation allowed a person to just "Be" – what a liberation that was.

He'd discovered fishing; though he'd been brought up by the sea he'd never bothered before, but now he understood that such an occupation was well suited to solitude and thought, and the early morning was ideal for the purpose. He narrowed his eyes as the bright sunlight glinted off the smooth golden surface of the water drifting lazily in and out of the rocky inlet where he was fishing. There was a slight haze this morning as the night air was warmed by the early sun. His peaceful contemplation was ended when he heard someone call his name, he turned to see Aidan walking with some haste towards him and waving something in his hand. Oswald laid his fishing pole down and stood, shading his eyes with his hand, he tried to see what Aidan was waving with such urgency.

Aidan and Oswald had become close friends over the last years. Aidan was older, but that didn't seem to make any difference. At first it had, in the beginning Oswald was a little intimidated by him, thinking Aidan aloof, but he discovered that Aidan was in fact shy and preferred to be quiet, actually *needing* time on his own. The years together had slowly moulded them into a pair who understood each other and their friendship had deepened.

'Brother Aidan,' he called, 'why such haste at this early hour?'

'The Abbot has had some news, and I was told to bring it to you with all haste,'

'News!'

'Yes, from Dunadd, a boat towing a barge loaded with timber arrived last night they unloaded and brought this document, but it never reached the Abbot until this morning he'd spent the night in prayer and fasting. He has only the hour past read it and sent me with it for your immediate attention.'

'Sit down my friend, it must be of some importance to take you from your early morning vigil.'

Aidan slumped down on the rock and passed the parchment to him wiped his brow and lay back, propped up by his arms. Oswald took it, sat next to him, and unfolded the missive.

'Mmm,' he frowned as he read it. 'I am to return to Dunadd. Finachnae mac Báetáin [19] some called him Fiachnae Lurgan; High King of all Dalriada [21] is raising an army to attack King Edwin at Bebbanburg. I know of this High King, but I've never seen him, he was a constant thorn in my father's side.'

'Yes, I know of him too, he comes from the north-east of Hibernia my homeland, and is part of the same family as King Eochaid Buide here in Alba, which is all part of the one kingdom of Dalriada. The Abbot told me that he thinks that your brother Eanfrith will see this as an opportunity to rid himself of the usurper King Edwin, regain his throne and take the gospel to Bernicia.'

'Mmm, I imagine so,' Oswald pondered, wondering what implications this would have for him. As far as he knew, he'd never met his uncle Edwin and had to confess to a certain curiosity about the man. He couldn't help wondering if his uncle knew the tale of his parentage and what had become of the great Wulfstan and Queen Aefre.

'Wulfstan and Aefre,' he spoke softly their names and felt suddenly – unaccountably sad for this mysterious couple that had lost their lives because they'd loved each other.

'The Abbot sent me; the curragh is yet waiting to take you to Dunadd. If you wish to go with them, you must make haste.'

'I must go, if this is truly a chance to regain our lost kingdom, we are bound to take it. I'm not sure that will be how King Lurgan sees it. Why would he risk his men for our sake? I doubt Eanfrith has given that question much thought.'

'I cannot say, but Oswald... I would counsel you to be cautious, the High King is powerful and I've heard he's cunning.'

Both rose to their feet, Oswald paused for a moment and stared out to sea, turned, nodded to Aidan and they set off towards the monastery at some pace, leaving his fishing pole where he had laid it. So, *this* was how it was to be, called into service to restore a kingdom of flesh and blood rather than the kingdom of his new master. How quickly the peacefulness of contemplation is broken when a war is declared.

'Oswiu must come too; we will pack quickly and go. I wish you were coming Aidan,' Oswald added as they walked. 'Who knows when we will meet again?'

'*God* does my friend, He knows everything He is never surprised,' Aidan said stumbling as he stepped on a stone with his bare foot. 'Unlike me,' Oswald caught his arm and steadied him.

143

'I should not imagine that an army would wait for the two of us even though we are Princes of Bernicia. Will you explain to all our friends here, especially Brother Darragh, that we did not have time to say farewell?' Oswald asked puffing.

'Don't be anxious, my friend – I will attend to everything – never fear. You must go now or you will not reach Dunadd before dark.'

Oswald rushed into their rooms shouting for his brother. 'Oswiu, Oswiu,' Oswiu ran into the building behind him.

'What's happened? I was outside in the garden and I heard you shouting.'

Oswald stopped halfway up the stone steps to their rooms, '*Oswiu*, thank God, come pack your possessions, as quick as you can I will tell you as we go.'

Oswiu did as he was bidden without question, and followed Oswald up the stairs to their rooms. They began to fill bags with their clothes and belongings. Finally, Oswald took a deep breath, and buckled his sword to his side.

Aidan was at the door as they came out loaded with their bundles and he embraced them both.

'Can you manage, do you need me to carry anything?'

'No, no, it's not far to the shore Aidan, we will be alright.'

'I will, pray for you both, I promise you. May God go with you, and be assured of my *daily* prayers.'

'Thank you Aidan, I will miss you. Come Oswiu, down to the beach, Aidan says the curragh is waiting.'

Aidan nodded, 'Go.'

The two ran with their belongings the short distance down to the curragh. When they reached it, they waded into the water, the boat was already bobbing free of the shore.

They threw their belongings onboard and clambered in after them. No sooner were the two of them onboard, than the men pushed the curragh away from the beach with their oars and the sail was hoisted. It was instantly filled with an obliging gust of wind from the lee, which blew them into the open bay and away from the rocky outcrop.

'Now, are you going to tell me what this is all about brother?'

'Sit down and steady yourself first...' Oswiu seated himself as Oswald instructed, leaning back against the side. Oswald sat opposite him. 'King Finachnae mac Báetáin, do you know him?'

'I'm not sure, should I?'

'He's the High King of Dalriada from Hibernia.'

'Ahhh yes... I thought I'd heard the name before, didn't he fight against father?'

'Yes, that's him, he must be at Dunadd, we'll know better by nightfall. He is preparing warriors to march on Bebbanburg.'

'Will he want the sons of King Æthelfrith with him?'

'That was my first thought too. I suspect that he hopes that it might be to some advantage to have us with him when it comes to conquering the Bernician people and the fort at Bebbanburg. I doubt that he does it to restore the kingdom to the sons of his old enemy, if that's what Eanfrith expects and it may well be. Eanfrith wants Bernicia and that might cloud any clear thinking. We will just have to wait and see. I suspect that we'll have little choice either way.'

There were many ships of various sizes along the shore when they arrived at An Crìonan, but there was no one there to welcome the little craft this time as it ran up the beach, apart from the odd guard.

Oswald was first over the side leaping into the shallow water. Oswiu passed their belongings down to him, and then he too jumped from the curragh. They bade farewell to the men in the boat and made haste to the fort as best they could with their load, leaving the crew to secure the boat.

The guards at the gate recognised Oswald and Oswiu, so they were able to run into the fort unimpeded. They ran up the steps onto the highest level where they knew Eanfrith was most likely to be. There were warriors everywhere, laughing, talking, eating and drinking. Oswald was thankful that he could now at least understand their Hibernian tongue; he could see that such ability would be a great advantage if they were indeed to travel together and attack the Bernician capital.

'Where is Prince Eanfrith?' Oswald called to the first person he recognised, who happened to be the Briton Daffyd who Cedric had befriended; he was at this moment leaving the dunghole.

'Prince *Oswald!*' Daffyd looked surprised, 'Prince Eanfrith is in the longhouse, Lord, where I'm going,' he pointed. 'Come, I'll take you.' Daffyd signalled to a slave, the man came to him and Daffyd told him to see that the Prince's bundles were put somewhere that was safe for the moment. The slave bowed and Oswald and Oswiu passed him their belongings.

'Stay with them,' Oswald commanded him.

'*Oswald*, brother, good tidings, is it not,' Eanfrith rose unsteadily from his seat on seeing his two brothers entering the longhouse. 'I am delighted to see you, what do you make of this good news, brother? An invasion, all that we hoped for.' Eanfrith was in good humour, clearly the worse for ale; he even embraced Oswald and Oswiu. '*Ale* for these noble Bernicians,' he called out.

There were many new faces, which were unfamiliar to Oswald and Oswiu. Ale was passed to them and Eanfrith began to introduce them to the nobles around him. 'More good news too, I am to be a father, the gods have blessed me, a future king for Bernicia. What do you say to that?'

'The *gods*... What about your new faith?'

'Ahhh, who cares about the Christian God?'

Oswald looked at Oswiu, but said nothing. He hoped that Eanfrith might be in a more reflective frame of mind on the morrow.

Oswald guessed that King Finachnae mac Báetáin was the giant flame haired warrior surrounded by several important looking men, amongst them King Conadd Cerr and King Eochaid Buide. Oswald knew they would be stirring up the blood of warriors ready for the fight, with stories of great deeds of valour, and the promise of riches for all.

Oswald asked Eanfrith if Hrodulf and Cedric had been told of the gathering, Eanfrith said that they had been sent for and he expected them any day, probably on the morrow.

The place was mayhem, the noise was deafening and it had apparently been like this for days.

'You stay here Oswiu; I'm going to see if I can find Princess Helen,' Oswald shouted. 'Don't get drunk, you are not used to strong ale anymore than me. Remember how you felt that night on Coll when mother was laid to rest.'

Oswiu nodded, 'I shall not forget that in a hurry, I would have welcomed death's merciful hand, but it never came.'

Oswald could see how easy it would be to get caught up with the atmosphere in the hall this night, and live to regret it the next day. Oswald shrugged, resigned to what would be, he was about to leave the hall having asked several warriors and servants if they knew where Princess Helen was, when he spotted her sitting alone against the wall with her head between her legs.

'Helen, what's the matter girl?' she looked up, giving him a glazed look of utter bewilderment. She looked flushed and was sweating, he realised that she'd been one of the innocents who'd been swept along by the euphoria of the coming adventure.

'Oswald,' she said as he tugged her to her feet, slung her over his shoulder and carried her into the yard to the well, ducking her headfirst into a barrel of water. Her arms flayed wildly at the indignation and she struck him in the mouth with her fist, he immediately tasted the metallic tang of blood on his tongue.

The shock of near drowning was enough to bring her abruptly to her senses.

'Swald... they said you were here I never saw you,' Æbbe ran at him and almost knocked him over, fortunately he managed to brace himself in time to withstand the impact.

'Oswald,' Helen said once more, he and Æbbe knelt down next to her and she wrapped her arms around his neck, then pushed him from her, was violently sick, and collapsed into a heap on the ground sobbing and groaning as she held her stomach. He dipped a corner of her shawl into the barrel, sat by her side, rested her head on his lap and tenderly wiped her mouth and face. Once again, she clung to him and renewed her sobbing. He was content to hold her until she had calmed. Æbbe could do no more than look on unsure how to assist her brother.

'Oswald, I'm so sorry, I feel so ill.'

'I think that it's normal, but you will recover. There will be many who will feel as you do on the morrow, aye and far worse.'

'I do love you Oswald, I'm so pleased to see you, but I am ashamed for you to see me so.'

'I'm sure you are, it's not the welcome I'd expected, but don't worry I'm yet happy to see you,' and he smiled as he lifted her from the ground, cradling her in his arms. He carried her to her roundhouse, the place was empty, and he laid her on the first bed he found.

'Stay here, I will bring a maid to watch over you. You wait with her Æbbe, until I return.'

'Don't *leave* me Oswald!'

'I must, I will return in a short while, your father and brother will kill me if I'm found here alone with you,' he said looking down at this girl with totally different eyes, she was no longer a girl, but an extraordinarily beautiful woman, and she – loved – him.

Once Oswald was satisfied that Helen was safe, and cared for, he went to find Oswiu and was relieved to see that his experience on Coll had been remembered after all. It was a different story with Eanfrith; he was now laid under the table where Oswiu was seated.

'He's well enough Oswald,' Oswiu reassured him; I dragged him under the table for his own safety.

It was a greatly chastened Princess Helen Oswald was presented with the next morning. Oswald and Oswiu were among the rare early risers, there was food aplenty and they ate heartily before Oswald made his way to Helen's roundhouse.

The Princess was seated on a stool before her maid looking none too pleased to have a comb dragged through her tangled hair. She saw Oswald as he entered, but cast her eyes to her feet.

Oswald crouched down before her and looked up into her face.

'What must you think of me?' She said in a low quiet voice.

He took her hands in his, 'I think that I love you.'

She smiled, shook free of her maid and hugged him.

Chapter 14

Siege

The army made good time as it travelled southeast from Dunadd, Oswald and Oswiu had kept well clear of the leaders for most of the journey. Oswald settled in his mind that he would let Eanfrith enjoy all the adulation of being the Lord and King of the Bernicians. He didn't long for, or need any of that kind of thing; he knew such was a fickle measure on which to base one's self worth. He and Oswiu had both been made known to the High King and that was enough for them.

Oswald was as yet unsure of the High King's true intention – for the present – he would be satisfied with watching and listening, Brother Ségéne had always told him that it was no accident that God had given man two eyes, two ears and only *one* mouth. Clearly, the Christian God hoped that man should do twice as much looking and listening as he did talking.

The army was assembled for the night on the edge of the great purple moor with a view all the way down to the coast and Bebbanburg; it must be all of twenty leagues, thought Oswald. The view was magnificent and said all there was to say about why his heart loved this place.

There was much talking and good spirited humour amongst the warriors as they sat in their small groups. For this night, Oswald would be content to sit quietly rubbing his sharpening stone along the edge of his Ulfberht. He spit onto the stone once more, paused, and glanced up at Cedric, who was seated a little way from him with his forearm resting on his raised knee and his back against a large rock. He munched slowly and deliberately on an apple whilst gazing into the distance towards his home where he'd lived since he was a boy. The last six years away from his home he had only tolerated. Oswald tried to imagine what he was thinking. Every so often, he noticed that Cedric would massage his left arm and flex his fingers. Clearly, he was in some discomfort. Oswald wondered if he'd injured it on the way here, at least it wasn't his sword arm, which might have been a real problem. Men were going to die in a very short time and that would be all the more likely if a warrior was carrying an injury, especially in his sword arm.

Cedric being Cedric, he would never make a fuss over a simple pulled muscle, if that was what indeed it was, but it was clearly troubling him it hadn't been the first time Oswald had seen him doing this. He'd been quiet and at times irritable on the journey east, not like his usual self, for some reason he preferred to keep his own company.

Oswald had tried several times to engage him in conversation, but to no avail. In the end, he had left him in peace, but there was something disturbing him of that Oswald was *absolutely* sure. Oswald was far too close to him not to notice this strange uncharacteristic behaviour.

Oswald had asked Hrodulf if he knew what was troubling his friend, Hrodulf had merely shrugged his shoulders.

'Who knows, you know Cedric, he's not one to complain. He'll be fine, don't worry Lord, it's been a long journey and he's no young chicken, I'd guess he's tired like me.'

'Mmm,' Oswald knew all that Hrodulf said was true but it didn't satisfy him. No longer was Cedric the indestructible warrior of former days; it didn't take much exertion these days before he was panting like a winded old nag. Their roles were reversed now, Oswald wasn't exactly sure to a day when it had happened, but it for sure had happened.

He would watch out for Cedric, as Cedric had always watched out for him. That would be Oswald's work for the rest of Cedric's days, but Oswald knew that he would need all the skills and sensitivity he learned from his friend Aidan on Iona, to carry out that occupation with any measure of success. He knew without the *slightest* doubt Cedric would be at the *very* best difficult, if he thought that he was a burden to *anyone,* never mind to Oswald.

'He shouldn't have come Hrodulf, I tried to tell him, but I knew as I was speaking to him, I was wasting my breath. He was coming home to his "Din Guyaroi", as he ever insisted calling it, and that was the end of it.'

'I didn't even *try* to dissuade him Lord; we have been as one man for so long, if he is cut I will bleed and it is the same for him. That's just how it is when warriors become as close as we have been over the years, and closeness is invaluable in battle. So I know when to speak and when not to waste my time.'

'This I do ask of you Hrodulf, stay close to Oswiu and me, once we set off on the morrow, I want him near me every moment.'

'Do you really need to tell Cedric and me such a thing? We will die by your side. I thought you knew that,' and he slapped Oswald's back and he laughed. 'Awe, don't fret yourself, I understand your meaning.'

'Well, let us hope and pray that it doesn't come to anyone dying.'

It was a cool clear night and there were a million stars dancing in the heavens. Oswald could only stare in wonder at God's creation, as he lay with his head resting on his rolled up saddle blanket. God had spoken, and it was so, that is what the scriptures said.

Oswald prayed that the creator God, who had brought so much to his life, would be with them on the morrow in the battlefield where they would be faced with taking life away from his countrymen. Would the Christian God protect a warrior in battle? He had been confident that Wōden would.

He knew he must get some sleep, no one knew what the morrow held for them, but it would be all the better faced if they were not tired, and to that end he pulled his thick cloak over his head, prayed, and thought of Helen's tears when he'd left Dunadd.

She'd begged him not to go, but that was never a possibility, and he guessed, in her heart of hearts, she knew that, but it had been a difficult parting for both of them nevertheless. God willing, when he returned they would marry.

159

There was a fine mist when he awoke, not *too* bad, it would burn off once the sun got up, but it was enough to wet the belongings they'd left unprotected.

Oswald shivered as he pushed the damp cloak from his face, sat up, stretched and yawned. He was glad that he'd wrapped his sword in the waxed cloth he'd brought for the purpose. He'd never used his father's sword in a real battle, but Brother Ségéne said he was a born warrior, and that he'd never known anyone with his natural ability. Oswald knew that the next few days might prove the truth or lie of that high praise.

They ate the last of their dried meat; there were no fires, they didn't want to take the risk of being seen by any of the Bernicians loyal to Edwin, though none really believed their presence would have escaped the ears of King Edwin, no, Edwin would know.

Cedric was slow to rise, Oswald was watching him like a hawk, but no one made any comment. Oswald noted that he'd slept in his mail and wasn't sure how to read that, perhaps he wanted to be prepared for a surprise attack – or – more likely he was too weary to remove it and didn't want to have to go through the trauma of having to put it on this morning, exhausting his now limited recourses of energy.

'Remember, stay close to me young Prince and learn how a real man fights,' was Cedric's morning greeting. He actually smiled as he mounted his pony, which pleased Oswald. Oswald returned his smile and led his pony to where Cedric was waiting, he tapped Cedric's leg and beckoned him with a twitch of his finger, and Cedric leant down to him.

'How do you feel about making war on our own people, Cedric?' Oswald whispered.

'I will be fighting warriors who want to stop me entering my home, they will never be the Bernicians, I know.'

'That's one way of looking at it I suppose, I'll try to keep that in mind, though with a little effort, I may be able to pick holes in that argument.'

'Aye, I dare say, but you would be wise to heed my advice, you don't need confusion in your head when someone's about to gut you.'

Oswald smiled and nodded. He and Oswiu mounted their ponies and fell in behind Cedric and Hrodulf, as they headed down the long sloping road to the sea and

Bebbanburg. It would be midday before they reached to coast, no point in rushing, Edwin would see them coming.

It was King Finachnae mac Báetáin's intention to assault the fortress from the south seaward side; the walls were lower there. No doubt, Eanfrith had suggested that approach, but as they neared the beach, Oswald felt pangs of uncertainty about the decision, for there was little cover.

The fortress looked fearfully imposing before them as they dismounted. Oswald wondered if they would camp and attack on the morrow, but no, he couldn't believe it. They were unloading the ladders and scaling equipment and looked as if they were going to rush at he walls without the slightest thought or discussion.

'*Cedric,* this is madness, say something,' but it was too late for that.

There was a sudden yell and the warriors began to run with pole ladders towards the wooden walls. Oswald was compelled to run with them and was no more than a pace behind Cedric. He couldn't help notice Cedric's erratic gate, he was staggering and stumbling, he looked as if his legs were out of control he would fall any moment, Oswald was certain.

Another yell went up, 'SHIELDS,' it sounded even more frantic than the first, not a second too soon. The ladders were instantly abandoned as a cloud of arrows rained death upon them. Some were not quick enough and fell with the look of hedgehogs. Cedric fell head first into the sand, unable to raise his shield, but by some miracle, he was only struck with one arrow, a flesh wound in his shoulder, nothing serious.

Oswald, Oswiu and Hrodulf leapt as one to cover him with their shields. They stayed covered by their large war shields until the deluge ceased. Cedric never moved. Oswald dragged his arm from the straps of his shield.

'*Quick,* turn him over,' they did as Oswald said and Oswald rested Cedric's head on his lap, Cedric's lips were purple, he slightly opened his eyes and smiled at Oswald.

'It's over son...' he spoke in a whisper. His voice was so quiet Oswald had to press his ear to his lips to hear him, but then the words were only for him anyway. 'Never was a father more proud of a son,' his said in a whisper, he paused and gave a shallow gasp. 'You may not be my flesh and blood, but you're my son, right enough,' he coughed and a trickle of blood ran from the corner of his mouth, 'there will be more than me laid out in this sand afore the day's end, but I'm happy to lie here son. Mind – don't lie me next to one of them monk priests from Iona,' and he smiled weakly, coughed once more, closed his eyes, his lips moved, but there was no sound – it was over... Oswald was trembling, his teeth were chattering, he couldn't control himself.

Suddenly another cry went up, 'BEHIND US.'

Oswald shook his head and stared with disbelief, there seemed to be hundreds of warriors coming at them from out of the sand dunes. They turned as quickly as they could and tried to form some sort of shieldwall, but it was hopeless, King Edwin's men were upon them. The half formed shieldwalls fell apart, it was hand-to-hand fighting, Oswald and Hrodulf stood shoulder to shoulder and another warrior leapt next to them, it was Daffyd, and the three of them stood back to back and formed a triangle with Oswiu and Cedric in the middle. All Oswald's training and natural talent were needed for this; his first blooding. They fought for more than two hours; the sand was red with blood. Eventually, Edwin's men began to lose ground.

The four comrades had never moved from the spot, the dead were heaped around them. Finally, the Dalriadans began to take control of the ground and Edwin's men were forced to turn tail and run, but King Finachnae mac Báetáin had paid a terrible price for his rash assault on the fort.

Was it grief or exhaustion? Who could tell, but Oswald knelt, clasped Cedric's hand, pressed his forehead to his chest and wept unashamedly for the loss of his dearest friend. Hrodulf crouched next to Oswald put his arm around him and wept too.

All their vain hopes dashed in a single afternoon. After all the distance that they'd travelled, it was over in just *one* afternoon's fighting. Oswald could not believe the stupidity, or was it the arrogance of kings who believed their own lies, that they were wiser, and divinely greater than mere mortal men and certain their gods would be on their side because even they were dazzled by their greatness. That bloody lie, yes, and *bloody* lie it is, this red sandy ground bears witness to that truth, and is here for all to see how noble kings stand humbled by their vanity. Let them, who profess such nobility, fall prostrate before those who are subject to them, or at the very least hang their heads upon their chests in shame.

The darkness had lowered her sombre cloak upon this day's malediction, before Oswald was able to take in the true scale of the catastrophe. He didn't know how long he'd been sitting there. He'd never moved from Cedric's side he and Hrodulf were both seated together on the sand, simply staring at the body of their dead friend, oblivious to the hell world around them. Oswald looked up, and saw Eanfrith talking to Oswiu; he'd never given him a thought until this moment, but on seeing him, he was glad that he had survived, though at this moment he may well wish himself dead. There were groups of warriors all around standing talking, clearly almost as dazed as he was.

The next day was spent digging graves for some innocents to find in years to come, and wonder why so many bodies were buried there. The truth of the forgotten graves, would be that history had not time to record the slaughter upon her slate so fleeting was the moment.

Oswald and Hrodulf laid Cedric to rest, and Oswald lashed two pieces of driftwood together to make a cross, and hung upon it the Thor's hammer, which Cedric always wore around his neck. Oswald remembered Cedric saying that he would let the god's

166

decide who welcomed him into their hall; it was all down to their charity in the end.

It would be as he wished, but Oswald would pray a Christian prayer that one day he would have a proper grave in a Christian holy place, and there he would rest until the final day of resurrection. [23]

The Dalriadans withdrew to safer ground to decide on the future of the expedition. It was decided by the kings that their numbers had been so depleted that any chance of victory was now hopeless.

Eanfrith stormed out of the tent, he was furious, cursing and swearing, and slashing with his sword at anything in his way. Oswald was concerned and understood Eanfrith's utter frustration and the despair that he felt, at possibly never regaining his kingdom.

Oswald would go to him when he'd calmed and endeavour to inject some hope into his despair.

Chapter 15

The Unforgiving Master

Before Oswald this day was a more subdued band of warriors than the ones he had seen, but a few days past, in the great hall at Dunadd. Those warriors were drinking and feasting, they were giants amongst mere mortals; nothing could ever bring those warriors to their knees.

It was *difficult* to believe that these bedraggled specimens of mankind; *he* was now a *part* of, were the same people as those drinking and feasting warriors; giants amongst mere mortals whom nothing could ever bring to their knees. It was a heartbreaking, miserable sight, to see these defeated and broken shadows setting their foot on the road back to Dunadd and shame.

These three kings were not carrying gifts heralding the birth of a new and glorious kingdom; they were not even riding near to each other. This disaster had driven resolute wedges of blame and contempt between them.

Then there was Eanfrith... poor Eanfrith; Oswald's heart reached out to him, for he wore the heavy mantle of rejection, even his own people hated him or he thought it to be so. In the evening he sat alone, he was at this moment no more than the feral wolf, separated from the pack, left to die, knowing that he was not wanted and detested by all. He was the embodiment of their tribulation, the living-breathing reminder of their tormentor, the *King* of *Bernicia*.

Oswald tried several times to talk to him, but Eanfrith didn't want his comfort at any price. He saw Oswald's attempt at kindness as no more than cynical mockery, delighting in his suffering. Oswald thought it the saddest thing for a human being to actually think he deserved the cruel treatment he was given. Wasn't that a lie to be fought in the heads of the followers of the Christ – that they were unworthy of forgiveness and redemption? He knew that one thief on his cross at Calvary had accepted Christ's forgiveness and the other rejected it.

Both might well have deserved all that was meted out to them, "But" that was not the issue, the issue was, were they prepared receive the undeserving forgiveness that the Christ God was offering? Only one of the two thieves was humble enough to reach out and take the gift.

Always a simple choice, the two trees in the garden, good or evil, light or darkness, truth or lies, life or death, Barabbas or Jesus. Brother Ségéne said that all down through the ages God yet offered man that simple choice, the Christ God, or the world.

Eanfrith simply could not grasp hold of that hope. He could not, or would not, see the mutilated hand of the Christ God reaching out to him, and was content to wallow in the misery of his human condition.

Oswald recalled that Brother Ségéne had often said, failure put a man on his knees, but defeat left a man face down in the dirt. Not only Eanfrith was in such a place of desolation at this moment, it was the condition of the whole army.

Those who were yet able, would have to raid and forage as they went on their way, and pray God, that they showed mercy to those who could no longer fend for themselves. Oswald knew that victory had many fathers but defeat was an orphan.

All had been brothers as they travelled south, but now Oswald saw only orphans without any family connection to the land of milk and honey. It had not yielded its riches to these warriors from the north, not – as they'd expected. There was no milk, for the pasture had been scorched by the heat of man's impulsive folly, and the honeybees searched in vain for a flower, which had not been corrupted by the stench of fresh blood.

Oswald wondered if King Edwin had any idea whatsoever that his nephew had been at the gates of his fortress, or if he even knew of his existence.

Out of the blue Oswald wanted to know every detail of the lives of his mother and father, Aefre and Wulfstan, but it was too late, their tale had been laid to rest with

Cedric, now no one would ever know the truth, it would be hidden in the folds of the shroud we call history.

The mighty fort of Bebbanburg was yet clearly in view when Oswald drew his pony to a standstill, he stared at the reins in his hands resting on the up-stand of his saddle. Oswiu came to him.

'What ails you brother, you're not carrying some hurt are you?'

Oswald lifted his head and stared at him.

'Hurt...? Aye, and deeper than any slash from a war axe, or even from the keen edge of an Ulfberht.'

Oswiu nodded slowly with heartfelt understanding, 'You refer to Cedric; I take it, brother?'

'Aye – Cedric – and I have had a hundred other nicks to my heart these past days. This is our home Oswiu, this is where we belong, these are our people, and we may never see this place or them – again. The pain is hellish and it consumes me.'

'Is there a problem, Lord?' Hrodulf's voice broke innocently into Oswald's grief, lacking any awareness of his condition at this moment.

Oswald responded without turning to him, 'I'm going back, Hrodulf!'

'Back... back where? Not to Bebbanburg!'

'Aye.'

'No Lord, I forbid it,' and Hrodulf snatched the reins from Oswald's hand startling Oswald's pony, which skittered and tugged at the rein.

'You forbid it! I must, I need to be alone and say goodbye. I will soon be with you again, fear not, but I must do this.'

'No, I cannot allow it, if you go I'm going with you, Lord.' Hrodulf's pony twisted and turned as if it was part of his anxiety.

'You are a good man Hrodulf, but I need to do this and do it alone,' and he gently reached across and withdrew the reins from Hrodulf's hand.

'Lord – I beg you not to take part in such folly...'

'Did you not hear me? I have got to, Hrodulf.'

'If that be your resolve, I will wait here until you return. I will give you one day only – then I will come for you. If you place any worth on my miserable hide, you will return before the day is out. Let that consequence be upon your conscience.'

'You are a rebellious huscarl to threaten your Lord and master so unashamedly, but if you insist, so be it.'

'Hrodulf's right Oswald, it is foolishness, but I do understand. I will wait here too; remember Eanfrith and me, and what about Helen, how would your careless folly satisfy her? At the very least think of her, if your thoughts extend to no other.'

'I must do this, for the very reasons you say I should not. I'll return, you can pray for me, Oswiu. Remember that incredible gift that is ever at hand.'

With that, he tugged on the reins, the little pony resisted but for a second, and then obediently turned back towards the fort.

Oswald walked his pony in the shallow water as it rolled gently up the sand. Though he could readily see the fort over his left shoulder, there was no sign of any action that might endanger him. They were sure to have seen him. He wondered if the very boldness of his lone appearance caused them to suppose that this was some sort of trick. Perhaps they thought his mount was not flesh and blood but a wooden horse, the like of the beast in Helen's tale of a horse filled with men about to sneak into the fort, and overwhelm them. For whatever reason, there was no sign of activity, threatening or otherwise.

He rode to the far end of the beach to the black rocks, dismounted and sat down upon them. He stared at his home, never blinking, as if trying to burn the sight before him into his thought world, every slope, tuft of grass and stone, imprinted forever. When he was satisfied, he mounted and rode once again along the beach, past the fort and on into the dunes to the holy place where his dearest friend lay. He slipped from his pony and quietly knelt by the grave for some time, and finally he closed his eyes and began to pray...

'Fæder ure þu þe eart on heofonum... [24]

Hallowed be thy name, Thy kingdom come, Thy will be done, on earth as it is in heaven.

Give us this day – our daily bread, and forgive us our wrong doings as much as we forgive others.

Lead us not into temptation, but deliver us from the hand of the evil one, for Thine is the kingdom the power and the glory forever and ever, without end. Amen.'

He slowly opened his eyes, it was almost dark now, he didn't realise he'd knelt there for so long. The fort was slipping from his sight in every sense. He mounted once again and returned to where he'd left Oswiu and Hrodulf. They stood when they heard him, Oswiu ran to meet him, and Oswald slowed and walked his pony wearily towards them.

Every homeward step was a miserable one; the weather even reflected their misery for it rained incessantly. There were daily fights and arguments between the men. Wounded men died and sickness began to spread amongst the defeated warriors as untreated wounds became putrid and their suffering was increased.

Oswald found little comfort in that his part in the conflict had been noted and those who were witness to his courage as a warrior began to call him by the Hibernian name of Lamnguin or "Whiteblade" [25] because of the way the light flashed off the blade of his Ulfberht in the heat of battle.

At last, the fortress of Dunadd was in view, Oswald was torn as they approached. On one hand, he was pleased that he would be once more with Helen, but on the other, there would be a reckoning for their failure, maybe even war throughout Dalriada. One thing Oswald was sure of, this debacle would not obligingly drift away from the memory of the families who'd paid the ultimate cost, of the life of a loved one.

The praise and deference he was being subjected too did little more than embarrass him. That people older and with years more experience should bow to him was not right.

Hrodulf had tried to explain to him, that people were suffering unbelievably and they needed something of worth to hang onto and identify with.

'At this time Lord, the gods have chosen that to be you, and you will have to learn to live with it. I have known men it has destroyed because they began to believe that they were above others. Guard against that Lord.'

'I hear you Hrodulf, I commission you to be the weight around my ankles.'

Hrodulf smiled, 'I think you know Lord I am equal to that task,' and he reached across to Oswald and they clasped hands. 'This will be your first test, no cheering as we enter I notice, bad news travels faster than a straight arrow.'

If anything Hrodulf was overestimating their welcome, women and children scuttled out of sight, fearful of what would happen now the army had returned.

King Eochaid Buide dismounted and looked around the yard, eventually a stable boy came hesitantly to take the rein of his horse. On another day, the King would have severely upbraided the boy for his tardiness, but today he merely handed the reins to him and said naught.

Oswald looked around, expecting to see Helen; she must surely know they had returned... he twisted in his saddle, she was there, a door only just opened and he saw her beckon him. For the flash of a single moment he forgot all about his aches and pains, he swung his leg over his pony's head and slid his bottom from the saddle. Glanced around the faces of the jaded warriors and made his way casually to the roundhouse. The door opened before him and closed as if by magic and he felt her lips press to his. Oswald wrapped his arms around her and she pressed close to him arching her back. He tenderly kissed her throat and she melted as she felt the tension of days of anxiety fall away from her. They had spoken not a word of greeting; their lips said all there was to say. Helen laid her head against his chest.

'I have missed you my beautiful warrior, thank God He saw fit to wrap you in His arms and keep you safe.'

'It was hellish Helen, the whole adventure was a disaster from the moment we got to Bebbanburg.'

'We know, riders came the day past and told us but we were also told of our new hero for all to sing of in new spun ballads.'

'Hero!'

'Oswald of Bernicia you fool, he was all the messengers could talk of once they made known to us the terrible losses. This Oswald killed one hundred warriors by himself, they were but flies before his "Whiteblade", so we were told.'

He laughed without humour; 'the number has doubled since we left Bebbanburg.'

She laughed too.

The laughter drained from Oswald's face as he spoke... 'Cedric died,' she pushed against his chest and stared in disbelief.

'My dearest Oswald,' she lifted herself up wrapping her arms around his neck and pressed her lips to his cheek. 'I am so sorry, he was your father, I know the love between you. What happened, were you there?' She took his hand and they sat on some sacks of grain, 'Tell me.'

He leant forward resting his elbows on his knees and hung his head. Helen pressed close to him gripping his arm.

'Yes, I was there, I was following him, we were running up the sand dunes, it was utter folly, it all just happened. It was exhausting, even my legs were on fire, and then to make things worse they released a hail of arrows that fell from the sky like a black cloud of death. One struck his shoulder, but it was only a flesh wound, nothing really it barely broke the skin. Suddenly he began to stagger and stumble, it was most odd, and then he folded forward into a heap,' Oswald's voice trailed off to a whisper... 'He couldn't go on, Helen, he tried to raise himself, but he couldn't, he tried, he really tried Helen, but he couldn't. All he said was, "It's over, son".' Oswald cupped his face in his hands and slowly shook his head; Helen hugged him and cried too.

After a time Oswald wiped his face on his sleeve and sighed, 'Thank you Helen, I thank God daily for you. You have been here for me from the very first night I arrived, that is a very precious thing.'

'Not really, I knew I was going to marry a hero, who slew two hundred giants with a single flash of his blade.'

Oswald smiled at her attempt to bring some cheer to him and he kissed her once more. Helen released him and lay back on the sacks and Oswald looked down on her.

'Will you marry me? Princess Helen of Dalriada.'

'I will, Oswald Leodwalding of Bernicia.'

'I will have to speak with your father and perhaps Eanfrith, but first I want to return to Iona and see Brother Ségéne and Abbot Fergno, would you mind if I did that?'

'Not at all, but I'm afraid we have had news that Abbot Fergno has passed away. Brother Ségéne is now the Abbot.'

'Really, this is a time of great change, Brother... Abbot Ségéne for ever would say to me, that God never awakes in the morning and is surprised by the days event.'

Oswald had talked to Princess or *Queen* Edlin, as Eanfrith insisted she be called, but she'd said that Eanfrith had barely spoken ten words to her since he'd returned from Bebbanburg.

Oswald tried to explain to Edlin how Eanfrith thought and why he'd felt as he did. After all, at this point in time, it must look to him as if his kingdom was gone from his reach for ever, and the truth, as painful as it was, might well be that it had indeed gone forever. It was a little easier for Oswald at this moment, because he had his forthcoming marriage to distract him, but he knew that when he reflected, as no doubt Eanfrith did, on what the future might have in store for him, and the kingdom of Bernicia, his mood was none too different to Eanfrith's miserable condition.

There were no tears this time from Helen when he set sail for Iona, as she would be fully distracted preparing for his return and their wedding. In fact, on this occasion, she nearly pushed him into the curragh. They both laughed and kissed. She still waved until she could no longer see him, then she ran home.

Her cousin Queen Edlin would be like a mother to her in this time of preparation and Helen vowed she would enjoy every moment. Oswald would never regret that *she* was his wife.

Helen shared Edlin's sorrow for her husband, but Helen was sure he would get over his disappointment *and* he may well yet be King of Bernicia. It was confusing to her for Oswald had said that he was not in fact entitled to call himself King, not until the Witan had decided and they made him their King. At this time, he was no more than a de facto king, and for all his assertions, Oswald knew that Eanfrith understood that, but for now, he must move on.

Both Oswald and Helen were surprised how quickly the adventure had been forgotten. King Finachnae mac Báetáin had returned to Hibernia and slowly the fort was returning to something approaching normality. Oswald prayed that King Edwin might not allow his victory over the Dalriadans to make him over confident, and imagine that he would attack King Eochaid Buide and conquer Dalriada. Thus adding to his empire, but for now Oswald had other concerns he was slightly nervous about meeting his old friend, wondering if he had changed with his new position.

Oswald leapt from the curragh, it had become a well-practiced manoeuvre and walked on up to the Monastery.

Chapter 16

Abbot Ségéne

Oswald knocked nervously on the worn oak door just below the familiar well polished brass cross, where countless knuckles had no doubt rapped over the years, fearing as *he* did at this moment, that

184

they were to be admonished for some infringement of which they were *ever* guilty, being part, as they were, of God's fallen creation.

A monk opened the door just enough to see who was there.

'Ah... Prince Oswald, it's yourself then, is it not, come in, come in,' the rather small young man said with a strong Hibernian accent. 'It's fine to see you again, so it is, you have been expected so you have.'

Oswald smiled at the young man whom he'd known and liked, for several years. The Abbot's room hadn't changed since the last time he'd been here to see Abbot Fergno.

It was plain with whitened walls and a well-polished wooden floor. There was always a sort of sweet musty smell about the place, but it was yet warm and inviting. On the wall by the door where he'd entered, hung a large wooden cross facing the Abbot's work table, which was covered, just as it was in Abbot Fergno's day, with rare books, parchments and writing materials. In the wall adjacent to the table, there was a glazed window overlooking the bay. No doubt, it served to give an inspirational, if somewhat distorted view of the world outside, for it was difficult to make out much if anything that lay beyond it, but at the very least, it provided some light for the Abbot to see his writings.

'Welcome Prince Oswald, be seated,' the voice said, as the smiling face of Abbot Ségéne, [8] looked up at him. 'You may leave us brother Darragh,' the monk smiled once more at Oswald, genuflected before the cross on the wall, and left. Opening and closing the door, with such practised skill that the only sound was the faint whisper of the hem of his habit brushing over the floor.

Oswald sat on the bench in front of the table. The friendly welcoming face of the new Abbot set Oswald at his ease.

'I am delighted you could come Prince Oswald, I longed to see you and hear your news, this is the first chance we have had to talk together, and renew our old friendship since your disappointing travels to your home land. As you can see I have now become the Abbot of Iona.'

'Should I congratulate you Father?'

The Abbot laughed, 'To early to say my son, perhaps no one else wanted the work.'

'I know better, as do all who live and serve here. I consider that I have been fortunate during our time together to have learned much from your wise counsel.'

'You are kind; Abbot Fergno talked a great deal about you, before he died. He had huge hopes that you might one day take the

Gospel of Christ back to your own land of Bernicia. Did you know this?'

'He made some mention of such, but I never took him seriously.'

The Abbot lifted his eyebrows, but made no comment. 'How old are you now, Oswald?'

'I'm eighteen, Father.'

'It seems a long time since you first came to Iona, you were a pagan then.'

'Yes.'

'Are you continuing as strong as ever in your faith, after... what is it, six years?' The Abbot asked glancing at a parchment before him and focusing on the date written there by touching it with his forefinger. 'Though you do not come so often now, you are always welcome.'

'Thank you Father, yes, I came here first in 617, not long after I arrived with my family at the Dalriadan court. I *should* say – I'm yet a Christian, Father, I suppose I am anyway. I have been baptised, and follow the Christ's teaching. Sadly, that forever annoyed my friend and mentor. There was never a man, I would set above him as an example of how one should live one's life, save you Father,' the Abbot's eyes lit up as he smiled.

'You do me great honour to number me alongside your friend, whom you held in such high regard.'

'He was a man, who actually lived by the ideals of what *you* teach here, though he worshiped Wōden, and I doubt he would ever have seen the need to convert to a lesser, *weaker* god as he understood the Christian God.'

'A *weaker* God you say!' The Abbot asked lifting his eyebrows once more, 'I should have liked to meet such a man,' he continued with obvious sincerity.

'I would have like that too. I asked him to come several times, but he would not. He always said *he* could have taught me all I ever needed to know, and my time here was naught but to humour King Eochaid Buide and those of his Dalriadan court, and it served only that purpose, no more than that.'

Abbot Ségéne smiled, leaning back in his chair, 'and what do *you* think, Oswald of Bernicia?'

Oswald hesitated for a moment, *what did he think...* that was an interesting question... 'I have learned how to read and write, understand number and to speak Hibernian, and it is with all gratitude to you Father.' Abbot Ségéne sitting back in his chair with his hands on his chest, and his

188

fingertips pressed together, bowed his head in acknowledgement of Oswald's kindness. 'I can see the value of such ability. I will never doubt that the Christian God is the only true God, I daily grow closer to Him, and I am told that He died for my sins, but what that means is as much of a nonsense to me as it ever was, the more I think about it the less I understand it. My friend Cedric told me that Wōden rewards us with an afterlife too, without the peculiar need to be killed and then to rise again. No one can kill Wōden in the first place, or so my friend would say. Who then is the greatest? It is said that my father Æthelfrith massacred 1200 Wealas Christian monks who had gathered to *pray* to their God against my father's victory. I don't know how truthful that number is, tales and numbers often grow with the telling.'

The Abbot smiled sadly, and shrugged his shoulders. 'Yes, I remember Augustine's grim warning when he said, "if the Wealas don't wish peace with us; they shall perish at the hands of the Saxons".'

'But what does that say about the Christian God's ability to stand against the followers of Wōden? I have found that to live a life worthy of the "Great Hall", always brings respect from the best of men. Men whom I hold as good men, who have

189

lived honourable lives, *such* is the life I would hope to live. Cedric, the friend I speak of, said that the gods could argue amongst themselves who would welcome him into their homes when his time came, there is little he could do either way, it would be down to their charity in the end.'

The Abbot listened intently, struck by Oswald's bold honesty and self-confidence. He was clearly a young man who had thought about life and was not afraid to voice his opinion, and not in a defensive arrogant way. The Abbot knew from the past, Oswald was open and equally responsive to sincerity and honesty. He would be no blind follower who believed everything he was told on face value. What was said had better stand up to the vagaries of this world. Abbot Ségéne pitied the teacher who was standing before this young man and was not teaching from a position of deep personal faith, but he'd always known that about Oswald. He was no ordinary young man; if it had been his calling, he would have been the Abbot of Iona. This young man had the mark of greatness upon him; Abbot Ségéne was not in the slightest doubt of that, and yet he was blest with the grace and humility, which would never yield such presumption.

The Abbot now leant forward, rested his elbows on the table before him, and steepled his fingers lightly against his lips, hesitating for a moment before he spoke...

'Mmm, I have it in my mind that when we face the Creator of the world to be judged, as surely the Holy Scriptures tell us that one day we will, one fellow will say, "I am a follower of Jesus," and God will ask him if he is such a man, why did he kill the innocent? Why did he steal food from the hungry? Why did he lie, cheat, and undertake all manner of calumny against his fellow man? Then the Judge of all may well say, "Depart from Me, I never knew you". There may be another who stands before God, having come through the same door as the previous fellow, for there will only ever be one way to enter into the Father's presence. That we may be able to come near to the Father was made possible at a fearful cost. He might call the Father of all by another name, for example, "Wōden", but it may just as well be a name not yet thought of, and the Father of all may see in the man's heart His own reflection, and welcome that man into His eternal presence. It is my humble opinion, for my opinion is worth no more than yours, that it is not what we say that defines us, my dear Oswald, but what we do. In the book of the most holy Saint James, it is written, in essence, what we believe in our hearts will determine how we live out our lives. Perhaps it is possible that the truth is sometimes written upon a man's heart, but he does not recognise the writer. What do you think?'

Now it was Oswald's turn to smile, 'I think my friend Cedric, the man of whom I have already spoken, would have done well to meet with you, Father, for he had said the same thing to me many times. Perhaps he worshiped the same god as you, when all is said and done.'

'Perhaps he did. I would very much like to have met this man. Now, may I ask, how are your brothers, are they men of established faith?'

'Who can truly see into the heart of another, Father, for sure I cannot?'

'Very true, my son, very true, out of the mouth of babes and children... you shame me,' the Abbot laughed heartily.

'For what it is worth, in truth I'm not sure what Eanfrith truly believes, he has been baptised, as you know, if that is the measure of a man's belief, but he never talks about his faith. Oswiu and I talk much about our new faith and our sister Æbbe loves to talk with us. She is Oswiu's full sister. We wanted her to marry Prince

Domnall Brecc, King Eochaid Buide's son, so that our two royal families may be more closely bound together. Eanfrith has already married one of King Conadd Cerr's daughters, Edlin, and they now have a son, Talorcan,'

'So I've heard.'

'But Æbbe would not hear of it. She said she wants to give her life to God. Perhaps the truth of it is that she didn't like the prince's freckles,' and both the Abbot and Oswald laughed.

'I hear also that you are to marry, is this so?'

Oswald blushed for no good reason, 'Indeed I am Father.'

'Then you have my blessing, it's not good for man to be alone, so the scripture tells us, unless your life is given solely to God as mine is. You have a different path to tread, I think.' The Abbot hesitated, then once more rested his elbow on the tabletop, and slowly stroked the curve under his bottom lip with the tip of his forefinger. 'I think my young prince, that you have an important future in service to the Church.' Oswald listened with intense interest, curious to know what the Abbot was about to say. Could God use a warrior as a missionary? Not being the king, or even of pure royal blood, he was not in a position to lead the people like King Eochaid Buide or even Eanfirth, should he be restored to the throne of Bernicia. Was the *Abbot* intending to raise an army, he wondered?

'You will find that the Church can be of great assistance and strength to those rulers who likewise give support to the furthering of the Gospel. Perhaps you will bear that in mind, "If" you decide to return to your kingdom of Bernicia.'

'I will indeed keep that in my thoughts, Father.' Oswald frowned and wondered if the Abbot's words were merely passing observations or a clear offer of support, but why make such a proposal to him rather than to Eanfrith. Was it possible that he had already had such a conversation with Eanfrith?

'I have heard tell of an island off the coast of... is it Bebbanburg, you call your capital?'

'Yes, some call it that now; to others it will forever be Din Guyaroi. The island is named Lindis Feorna, [9] by the Bernicians called by you Britons, "Metcaud".'

'Indeed, Metcaud, the very one, it is almost a perfect image of this island of Iona, I'm told.'

'Not quite, but there are similarities.'

'An ideal location for a Christian heart in which to take the good news to the pagans

194

of Bernicia, is it not? However, that is a thought for the future. I must thank you for coming to see me, Prince Oswald. I understand that you are unable to stay long on this visit, which is our loss; you have many who love you here and want to spend time with you. I hear King Eochaid Buide has a high opinion of you as a warrior prince. I have heard that they are calling you "Whiteblade", because of the flash of the steel from some mystical sword you own,' the Abbot laughed. 'I'm pleased that all my hard work was not in vain.'

'Yes, Father, that is true. As you know the sword was a gift from my father... He is part of it and lives in it,' Oswald answered as he rose from the bench. 'I have learned much from King Eochaid Buide, he makes his kingdom rich by trade rather than by warfare and expansion as my father King Æthelfrith did.'

'Always have an ear to learn, my son. You are joining us for our meal and staying the night with us I hope?'

'Indeed Father, but I must return to Dunadd with the morrows tide.'

'Thanks be, we will talk more this evening, you ever challenge my complacency. It is very easy to become accepting of the dogmas in a close community where one's beliefs are never challenged and refined. You are a breath of fresh air, straight from the Almighty Himself, my young Prince. I have missed you. Alas, there are very few who do not show complete deference to my opinions, wherever I go. Let my blessing go with you Oswald of Bernicia,' and the Abbot reached across the table and laid his hand upon Oswald's. 'May He who is able, keep and enrich your endeavours and straighten the path you set your foot upon, be with you and remain with you always.'

Oswald, bowed and kissed the Abbot's ring of office, rose from the bench and left.

Chapter 17

Bride and Wife

It had become Oswald's normal practice to rise before first light and find a space to be quiet, outdoors whenever it was possible, suited him best. It was simply how he lived; it had been a way of life for many years now. He'd discovered the disciplines of the monastic life were more than simple rituals; they had a valid claim to benefit man in all walks of life. Certainly as far as he was concerned, such time spent alone with his God helped clear his mind and set him on a right footing for the whole day.

This morning he was lying on the grassy slope that surrounded the high part of the fortress, and it suited his purpose perfectly. He could see over the ramparts and into the distance, for as far as his sight would carry him.

Suddenly his warrior instinct was awakened, he ceased his breathing and tried to slow down the beating of his heart. He became conscious of a barely perceptible change in the gentle whisper from the grass off to his left.

He understood more and more what Cedric had been teaching him since he was a boy, about the art and qualities of being a great warrior. "Awareness was the backbone of any great warrior's armour," he would say.

Oswald's hand lightly touched the hilt of his seax, and he tentatively caressed the smooth leather with his fingertips. He knew he could remove it from its sheath, and slice through a man's throat in the blink of an eye.

He turned his head fractionally and, to his relief, he saw no more threat than his young sister Æbbe coming slowly towards him, with a large smile on her face. Raising himself onto his elbows, he returned her smiled and she waved.

'Oswald, I have been looking for you and I caught sight of you up here. I was afraid that you were sleeping and I didn't want to wake you, I'm sorry if I have disturbed you.'

'Well here I am, you have no idea of the danger you placed yourself in sneaking up on me – and – when have you ever worried about disturbing me first thing in the morning, might I ask?' she laughed, for she knew as long as she could remember, her day had started by seeking out her brother Swald.

She sat down beside him, 'I'm sorry Swald but you did look to be asleep or in prayer, and truly I didn't wish to startle you. I would have waited quietly until you were able to talk to me. *But* forget all that, now I see you are indeed awake and this is a beautiful day – are you excited about this most important day, of days, Brother?'

'I am, what about you? Oh and please do be seated,' she laughed and pushed him. 'As a matter a fact, on this beautiful day, I was this moment thinking about *you* my dearest sister, if you must know.'

'You were! You're teasing me, I should think that your baby sister would be the last thought on your mind this particular fine morning.'

'It is the truth. I was thinking about you... I am concerned about your wish to join an order for women yearning to give their lives solely to God, known as brides of Christ. Are you yet certain that you want to give yourself wholly to God forsaking all others? You could have married Prince Domnall Brecc if you'd wished; he wanted your hand, you could have been a Queen one day, and yet still be a devout follower of the living God. In the role of Queen you could affect the lives of many by the choices made for your kingdom and changed them for the better.'

She smiled, 'You of all men should understand, that to give my heart to God will be as real to me as is your commitment to Princess Helen.'

'Yes... I understand that, believe me, but you are only twelve, are you certain what you feel is really a calling from God to join an Abbey? I don't mean to insult your sincerity, but there are many changes in your life at this moment, when you move from child to woman. Nevertheless,' he shrugged, 'you have time yet to change your mind. Have you talked to Eanfrith as head of the family?'

'*Eanfrith!*' she laughed. 'My dearest sweet Swald, you are so kind, to everyone; in fact you are the kindest person I know.

'Æbbe, your reaction was *unkind*, and you know it. Eanfrith tries and needs our support at this time not our mockery.'

'You're right, I'm sorry.' She said bowing her head. 'In all honesty, I have not spoken to Eanfrith, but let me settle your fears – the decision I have made – is the way for my life. I have thought of it constantly since you told me about your newfound faith. It is for me, my future is to give my life fully to God.' He looked at her and lay back, resting his head on his hands. Æbbe wrapped her arms round her knees and stared into the distance; they were silent for some time. 'I am honestly sorry I have disturbed you. I imagine you were with God. I'm ever selfish, forgive me, but I just wanted to have these last few moments with my big brother before his life changes forever.'

'I will yet be here my dearest Æbbe, I'm not going away,' she turned to him and smiled. 'Don't be afraid, Æbbe; none of us knows what is ahead of us. Fear enables some people and it disables others. I saw that when we fought at Bebbanburg, but I have a feeling that fear would not hinder you. However, my dearest Æbbe, much as I would love to sit here all day with you and chatter, I surely have other matters that make demands on me this day.' He leant over, kissed her, stood, and dragged her to her feet.

Oswald walked carefully down the incline, and leapt over a low chestnut paling fence, at the bottom of the grassy slope and lifted Æbbe over it.

'I will have to leave you now Æbbe, and ready myself to meet my bride, I would not like her to think that she is being joined to an impoverished beggar.'

'Not Helen, she knows she is marrying my brother, the most handsome man in the whole world,' she laughed, kissed him and walked off. Oswald watched her go, she turned fleetingly and he lifted his hand in acknowledgement.

Oswiu was waiting for him in his roundhouse, his clothes were hanging ready for him and there was a tub to bathe in, before he dressed.

'Ah, Oswiu... sorry I'm late, your sister wanted to talk. I will bathe and you can remind me of all I need to know.'

'There is plenty time. Abbot Ségéne, has arrived, he wishes to personally bless your union with the Princess. We came looking for you and wondered if you had perhaps run off,' Oswiu smiled. 'He is now with the King, Helen's father that is.'

'I wondered if he would come, that means a great deal to me, they must have sailed through the night. I hope that the priest here is not offended,' Oswald said as he climbed into the tub.

Eventually, after all the work and anxiety of the now tired servants, some of whom had worked through the night, *and* Oswald's restless pacing back and forth, for what seemed like hours... it was at last time – and the two young people faced each other, and held hands.

Oswald's eyes met Helen's; she looked very nervous, he thought, even more so than he.

She was indeed nervous, more than he could ever imagine, fearing that *he* might have regrets with his choice of a wife. At this moment, she was filled with self-doubt. She was endeavouring the best she was able, to hide her fears from all watching. She had wrestled all night with her worries about their union; she thought that she was perhaps not beautiful enough, clever enough, or interesting enough for a man of such increasing importance as he. He was now a hero, revered by men, a scholar, and handsome above any man she had ever known, whilst she was feeling, – so very plain and uninteresting, for such a man as this.

The eyes of this innocence girl staring fearfully at him, touched and warmed him, and he smiled, and in the tenderness of that smile all the words – she ever wanted to hear were spoken into *her* heart. She knew, and she would never doubt again, he *loved* her.

'He – loves – me,' she whispered under her breath. The tension drained from her, all she wanted at this moment, was to fall into his arms and dwell there forever.

Words were said and promises made, and then all of a sudden, she was conscious of the Abbot binding their hands together with his scarf and blessing them. She thought if heaven were more wonderful than this moment, leaving this world behind would be a glorious thing indeed.

The one dark spot on the day's celebrations was Helen's father, he was pale, and he looked so tired. Oswald knew that he'd not seemed well since they returned from Bernicia. That ignominious defeat had taken a heavy toll on him, as it had on all the other leaders. On the surface, it was if it had never been, never was it mentioned, not even in whispers behind closed doors.

Though there had been some "Slight" improvement with Eanfrith's health, he remained withdrawn. Oswald felt that the weight was shared unevenly by Princess Edlin, he was desperately sorry for the Princess, and felt that he should have been able to do more to alleviate her suffering, because he was after all, Eanfrith's brother. They had only recently been married, no more than some three years past, their son Talorcan was now toddling and trying to speak. This *cloud* of failure and depression tormenting Eanfrith was not even in the sky that day they were married, never mind constantly hanging over their heads as it now was.

Oswald had thought time and again, of the self-worth their marriage had brought to Eanfrith, he'd been a different man, until Bebbanburg... All had changed from that day, and he was now in a worse state of self-doubt, than he'd ever been.

Neither Oswald nor Helen guessed that within three weeks, her father would be dead and buried, and her brother Prince Domnall Brecc, would be the new King of Dalriada alongside King Conadd Cerr.

Helen was distraught when she was told. She and Oswald had been to see where his mother had been laid to rest on the island of Coll. It was important for Oswald to take her, and she wanted to go, never thinking that whilst they were away, her own father would die.

In some sense, there was even worse news to come; the Dalriadans were going to war in Hibernia, and Oswald would be expected to go with his followers, to fight against Maelcaich and the Irish Cruithne. The Cruithne were a people much like the Picts in their own land of Alba.

Ever since Oswald had fought at Bebbanburg, warriors had turned to him. Warriors would align themselves to any athelings that they thought worthy and able to advance them. Now that Oswald was the son of the King, his power and wealth had increased. Oswald was ever conscious of the threat he now posed to King Domnall Brecc, and King Conadd Cerr, though they never seemed to see it as a problem to them, it appeared as if they had complete trust in Oswald's loyalty. Oswald wondered if he would be so generous of spirit if he were in their place. However, they would expect his support now, and he would have to give it, which only served to cause more distress to Princess Helen, she'd convinced herself that Oswald would be killed and she would lose her beloved husband after waiting all these years to be together.

Oswald's faith in the goodness of God never wavered, 'God is daring us to trust Him, Helen. Trust that whatever circumstances unveil themselves before our eyes, that He loves us and that He will never flee from us. God will never leave us or forsake us, Helen. I am absolutely certain of this truth, and when you cannot believe this, let *my* faith uphold you.'

As with every war since the beginning of time, there was great activity prior to the event. Weapons were to be made and repaired; some stores were to be gathered, though they would forage for most of their needs as they travelled. More curraghs would need to be built, that was one of the beauties of the little craft, it was simple and quick to construct.

Oswald was now one of the respected leaders, which he thought absurd, but what he would bring to this venture would be a cool levelheaded approach. The folly of Bebbanburg would never be the reason his men died, *not* whilst he was in any form of command, and *that* he swore.

As the day for their departure approached, Helen could hardly eat or sleep. This was a level of anxiety she had never imagined possible. She endeavoured to hide her fears from Oswald, so that he might not be distracted, but she knew he understood, and his calm consideration for her was beyond any love she'd seen or known. This man's connection to his God was almost priest like.

Chapter 18

Warrior

Helen watched Oswald as he stared at the table, moving his food from side to side on his platter with the point of his knife. She was gripping her fists tightly under the table, pressing them into her lap, so that he would not be witness to her struggles and be distracted from his work.

Merciful Father, I can't hold my tongue. Help me, help me, I must be strong, the tension was travelling up her arms, she was shaking, he would notice, he must notice. *Help me* Father, she prayed.

She tried to breathe deeply and slowly. With all the strength she could muster, she asked, 'Is all ready for the journey on the morrow?'

He made no response; clearly, he'd never heard her, '*Oswald...*'

'Sorry, Helen... did you speak?'

She breathed deeply once more before she answered. 'I asked – if you were content that the army – was ready.' He still didn't look up. She sat waiting; his silence was the torment from Hell.

'You seem troubled, Oswald.'

'Do I? Mmm, in truth, I am troubled, I have little confidence in our leaders, they are not real warriors; they are traders. All I hear is indecision, sometimes I think that the only warriors here are Hrodulf and me.'

'But, you are one of the leaders, have you told them of your doubt and fears?'

'Both Hrodulf and I have tried to tell them, they listen, but are not able to hear; your brother Domnall Brecc is a fine man, but no Cedric or Hrodulf. Ohh, to have such a man with us, and King Conadd Cerr, if anything, is worse than your brother.'

Helen's shaking was now replaced by a limp despair; she was barely able to remain upon her seat.

'Will you still go?'

'Aye, I must, but I will make sure that my men are well led. We will not be slaughtered as we were at Bebbanburg. I'm already preparing for defeat before we set off, that does not bode well for us. Perhaps we will prevail and find that those who oppose us are led by incompetence as we are, but I fancy that will be a vain hope, for I have no faith in this venture. As you know the scripture teaches us that faith produces hope, all the hoping in the world will not produce faith.'

'Dear Father in heaven – how will I live until you return?' Helen cried.

Her heart now reached Oswald for the first time, and he looked up and smiled; now conscious of her fears.

'Forgive me Helen. I am burdening you with my selfish concerns, and filling your world with unwarranted doubt and fear, I will return and with an army, you can be assured of that. You must have no worries for my men, we will not turn from the fight, but we will not die mindlessly either. Pray for the others who are led by the two

Kings,' and he rose from his seat, went to her and embraced her, pressing his lips to the top of her head.

'I will pray for you all,' she said.

Come the morning light, the men and their families were on the beach, there were no ponies as the curraghs were totally unsuited to transporting them.

The plan was to sail up the River Bann as near as they could to the inland lake of Lough Neagh and then go on foot to Muine Mór. [26]

Oswald's fingers slipped reluctantly from Helen's and he walked into the water to the awaiting curragh. He reached up to the frame on the side of the boat, as he was about to haul himself onboard, he paused and rested his head against the side. Suddenly he pushed himself away from it, strode out of the water, and back to Helen, wrapped her savagely in his arms and kissed her, as if he would merge their spirits into one, to spiritually multiply their strength.

'I *will* be back, never fear,' he whispered into her ear. '*Remember* – if He is for us, none can stand against us,' he turned and waded once more into the water to the awaiting boat and slung himself up and into it, as easily as mounting his pony.

The friends and loved ones of the warriors watched the boats slip silently away from the shore, as they, like phantoms from the spirit world, were gradually swallowed up before their eyes, into the shimmering morning haze.

Helen stood alone, separated from the others. Æbbe had watched her for a while wondering whether or not to go to her. In the end, she'd decided Helen may well want to be alone with her thoughts at this moment, and she would go to her later.

Helen stared into the distance long after the crowd had dispersed. She swept strands of hair from her eyes, which had been disturbed by the light breeze and were now held to her face by her tears. She lifted her shawl over her head, to hide her private grief, and made her way slowly back to the fortress.

By nightfall, the army was in the mouth of the River Bann, and from there, they would travel south down the river, their curraghs were ideal for this purpose.

It was already dark and King Conadd Cerr wanted to press on, but Oswald argued that they were better to rest with the sea at their back and lie low for the night, then proceed cautiously on the first light. He said it was utter folly to drive an army forward in the dark, in what was unknown territory. He thought that they needed to travel the next stretch of their journey in the one day and with speed.

Any delay once they had set foot on the journey south would extend the time King Mael Caích had to decide how to defeat them.

The only advantage they had was surprise, to attack quickly, before the Hibernian Cruithne warriors had time to assemble a credible defence. Once they had started south, they *had* to complete the journey without any delay.

If they went on now, they would need to stop and rest and that would give the Cruithne time to prepare for they would soon know that they were there, and travelling south.

No, Oswald *insisted* once they started they must reach their destination with all haste and strike quickly. This was not a fortress like Bebbanburg, where it would have been wise to consider their options before they attacked.

King Conadd Cerr listened, but he would not be persuaded, they *would* go now and rest before the battle.

Oswald despaired, they had made his decision for him, and his only focus now would be the safety of the men who looked to him. He was compelled to trust their guides as they made their way towards the inland sea of Lough Neagh, for he'd never been to this place before.

At midnight, King Conadd Cerr decided they would rest, so that they would be fresh for the battle if it came on the morrow. He was told that they were yet some way from the great lake, not far from a place; the guides were calling Fid Eóin. [27] They drew their curraghs into the bank and pulled them ashore for the night. Once again, Oswald begged them not to take the boats out of the water, to refloat them would take time and time they might not have.

Oswald was *convinced* that the Cruithne people would have seen them by now, and King Mael Caích would most certainly have been told of their army. Oswald was furious; at what he thought was a gift to the enemy, this would give them vital hours. He knew that King Mael Caích would now have the advantage, extra time to assemble his forces and select the point of contact. With his already superior knowledge of the landscape, he would know every hill and vale to use to his gain.

In fact, all the advantages for battle lay with the enemy, whichever way Oswald though about it, all he could see was that they would be giving their enemy the upper hand. With every step nearer to the conflict, he became more certain of their fate.

Oswald and Hrodulf spent most of their night in preparation. They made sure that their men were all at the rear of the army and able to escape if they were attacked and overwhelmed, some even slept in the curraghs. Oswald was certain that any hope of surprise was now lost to them. He would leave *his* curraghs in the water with men guarding them. His men would not have to waste time in having to re-float them.

At first light, they began to ready themselves for the next stage of their journey. Oswald was anxiously trying to put himself in the shoes of King Mael Caích and think what he would do in the King's position.

Hrodulf knelt down next to Oswald, as he was speaking to the Briton Daffyd, and said in a low voice, 'They are here Lord; I know it, assemble the men around our boats, and have them prepare. I have no idea of their numbers, but I fancy they will outnumber us

216

or they would not be so bold as to attack us.'

'Hell's teeth, you see to that Hrodulf, I must warn Helen's brother King Domnall Brecc, *if* he will listen, the *fools,* they could get us all killed.'

'NO, he's not worth it, Lord! He had his chance, don't risk...' but Oswald had already gone.

Oswald had no sooner reached King Domnall Brecc, than suddenly they attacked, charging with their long spears as if men possessed. King Domnall Brecc was frozen in panic. Oswald grabbed the neck of his mail and literally dragged him choking and coughing, back to the river bank, and behind their shieldwall; they were the only ones in any semblance of order and able to offer some resistance.

Hrodulf had done well, his old friend Cedric would have been proud of him; Daffyd was also a man who knew his business, no wonder Cedric had liked him. Oswald pushed King Domnall Brecc to the ground and forced his way into the shieldwall.

This was Oswald's first shieldwall, but he knew what to do, he had stood behind the master and learned all there was to know; this was second nature to him.

217

There were just too many Cruithne warriors; the Dalriadans were being slaughtered. Oswald caught sight of the fallen King Conadd Cerr out of the corner of his eye; all that was recognisable was his torn purple cloak. His head had been almost completely severed.

It was all Oswald saw, a seax came over the top of his shield and nearly poked out his eye. He only managed to avoid it by a spilt second reaction, and at the same time that he ducked, he drove his Ulfberht underneath his shield and into the belly of his assailant. The man's eyes bulged in utter disbelief as Oswald dragged his sword free, and he slid down the front of Oswald's shield into a heap at his feet.

This sword came alive in this situation; its ability to bend was such an advantage in close quarter fighting. You could easily find a sword torn from your hand because of its lack of flexibility or even worse; it would shatter on the first contact with metal.

'Every second man drop out of the wall and close up, NOW!' Oswald yelled.

The ones who'd dropped out were to get the boats ready. The wall closed immediately they'd stepped from it, sealing the way to the boats. They had trained and practised all these manoeuvres in Dalriada, and they worked seamlessly.

Oswald had learned from the Bebbanburg disaster, that organisation and discipline was the way to win battles, and he'd decided that day, he'd not repeat the same mistakes of a band of warriors operating as individuals.

Oswald yelled again, 'every second man drop out of the wall – and close up, NOW!'

There were bowmen at this moment standing in the front of the boats. When the final men in the wall ran to the riverbank, they would be covered by them.

'NOW!' the wall broke for the final time and they backed as one to the boats, bending low so that the bowmen had targets. Swissssssh, an arrow shot passed Oswald's head so closely that the goose feather fletching brushed against his face.

The last men from the wall waded to the rear of the boats and climbed in, whilst the archers fired mercilessly into the men who came at them.

As they pulled into the centre of the river, Oswald could see that the Dalriadans they'd left behind were being slaughtered, but he had saved his men and others besides.

They needed now to make their escape up the River Bann, and return the way they'd come from the sea, and as quickly as they could.

There was nothing Oswald could do for those left behind, he could only watch. The only other option would have been to stay and die with them, a pointless death.

'You did well Lord, *he* would have been proud of you, I know it.'

'Thank you Hrodulf, but it need not have been like this, another utterly humiliating, stupid defeat, a total waste of life.'

'Aye... I know that, Lord, but take it from one who knows, every battle I have walked away from has been a victory, as far as I'm concerned.'

'Now that did sound like Cedric, that is something he would have said,' and Oswald gave a weak smile.

Hrodulf shaded his eyes with his hand, 'They don't seem to be following us. I don't think that they will have had time to organise a boom across the river to trap us, so we may be free.'

'Let's hope so Hrodulf, what a waste...'

King Domnall Brecc now stood and rested his arm on Oswald's shoulder.

'Sorry Oswald, we should have listened to you – *and* – thank you for my life. I will not forget the risk you took for me.'

Chapter 19

Land of the Living

Oswald led his men sombrely away from the shore and up to Dunadd, they were all that was left of the warriors who had gone to Hibernia, and died at the battle of

Fid Eóin. For such a number they moved silently.

The warriors dispersed, equally silently once they'd entered the fort, all but Oswald, he saw Eanfrith sitting on a bench at the door of his roundhouse. Eanfrith wearily lifted his hand in greeting and Oswald and King Domnall Brecc walked to where he was sitting and sat down beside him. Eanfrith made to stand, but Domnall touched his shoulder and he stayed seated. Eanfrith looked frail he had lost much of his strength and bulk because of his inactivity since Bebbanburg. He was clearly weak, but Oswald could see his health was improving the fact that he spoke to them, was a good indicator. He had on previous times; scuttled inside whenever someone went too near.

'How goes it Eanfrith?'

'I feel much improved Lord; it's good to see you Brother. No need to say ought, I can see that it did not go well for our army.'

'We missed your strong arm.'

'I'm strong right enough, at least in that I was, just like father, but you are *brave* that's the difference between us,' Eanfrith said in a soft resigned voice with empty eyes that stared straight through Oswald.

'You are too harsh on yourself, what happened at Bebbanburg wasn't your fault.

We were led by men who should have known better. Next time it will be different.'

King Domnall Brecc looked down, for he knew his father had been one of the leaders responsible for the shame at Bebbanburg.

'Do you think that there will be a next time, Oswald?' asked Eanfrith.

'For sure, and I would be your general if it was your wish. The King here has said, when we feel the time is right he will raise an army to help us regain what is ours.'

'You would do that for us Lord?' Eanfrith turned to the King in astonishment.

'I am now in Lord Oswald's debt and I will do my best to make right the grave state of shame I find myself in.'

Eanfrith visibly brightened at these welcome yet unexpected words of hope.

'I am learning much by the needless mistakes.' Oswald confessed to him, to add honesty to the encouragement. 'Mistakes can be a rare teacher, you learn, or you suffer, until you do, and I have been witness to many mistakes.'

King Domnall Brecc lowered his head once more, though Oswald had meant no insult or attempt at shaming him; he was merely trying to be encouraging to his brother Eanfrith.

As Oswald was speaking, he glanced over Eanfrith's shoulder and saw Helen step outside her doorway, no doubt alerted to the return of the army, by the disturbance and influx of warriors. She saw Oswald and quickly ducked back inside their roundhouse.

'I will leave you now, but we will talk later, I have just seen Helen behaving rather suspiciously.' The King turned to see where Oswald was looking.

'Yes, you should not be sitting here idly chatting with me, she'll think you are in no hurry to see her, and I'm guessing that falls short of the truth by the length of a straight arrow's flight.'

Oswald stood up stretched his neck from side to side and back and forth, it felt stiff. He'd pulled it to his certain knowledge when he dragged King Domnall Brecc to safety at Fid Eóin. He squeezed Eanfrith's shoulder and went to where he'd seen Helen.

He opened the door and walked in. She had been hiding behind the door and pounced on him, laughing with a mixture of raw hysteria, and relief.

'Oswald Leodwalding, how dare you keep us waiting. You can't imagine what it's been like, waiting here and not knowing. Was it a great victory?'

'Nothing like, we were slaughtered.'

'Dear God, what about my brother?'

'Fear not, he is safe, but his men suffered a mighty number of causalities.'

'But you escaped.'

'Yes, I was not about to see my men die for nothing, once was enough for me.'

'I prayed for you every moment, we needed you home safe and sound.'

'What do you mean, *we* needed you home?'

'Your wife and your son...' Oswald stared at her, his face was at first expressionless and gradually it was transformed into a smile.

'Did I tell you what a wonderful person you are? This is the best news to hear after all I have been witness to, believe me,' he said tenderly embracing her. 'When, will all this happen?'

'January next year, so I'm reliably informed.'

'Come, we must tell Hrodulf, who else can we tell, Eanfrith and Edlin, Queen Bebba, your brother and of course, Æbbe.'

'Actually, I have already told Edlin, I had to. I was so worried that I could not think straight, please forgive me.'

'Of course I forgive you, how could you suffer to keep this to yourself?'

Over the next months, there was more unrest within the greater kingdom of Dalriada; it seemed to Helen, her husband was constantly away from Dunadd she saw so little of him. Oswald Whiteblade's courage and leadership was on the lips of all, but that brought little comfort to her.

This was also a time of renewal for his brother Eanfrith who was once again fighting alongside him and Oswiu. Eanfrith would never inspire men like his brother Oswald, but for now, he seemed satisfied with this. Oswald thought the renewed optimism of returning to Bebbanburg had worked in him a message of hope and a future.

The hooves of Oswald's pony clattered on the stone steps up to the highest level of the fort at Dunadd. They'd never been intended for such a purpose, but Oswald drove the little animal up the incline onto the top and leapt from the saddle followed closely by Oswiu.

He had been out hunting with King Domnall Brecc, and his brother Oswiu, when a rider had been sent for him with news that his wife, Princess Helen, was about to deliver their child, and he was to return immediately.

He'd no need of direction he could hear Helen screaming before his feet had touched to ground. There were women milling around everywhere, he was forcibly barred from entering the birthing area.

'God in all His mercy, what are you doing to her?' he yelled.

'Be calm, brother nothing can be achieve by your distress,' Oswiu laid his arm on his chest and directed him to a chair.

The noise went on for hours, or so it seemed. Eventually there was a brief moment of silence, and then the cry of a newborn child was heard and he breathed the greatest sigh of relief, fell to his knees and gave thanks to God.

He was told that he had a son and all was well, he should wash and change ready to meet the newest member of the Leodwalding dynasty.

There was a tub provided and he was bathed, he merely lay in the tub with his eyes closed giving thanks to his God, and allowed the servant girls to do their work. Once the dirt of the hunt had been removed, he was dressed and taken to see his wife and new son.

The cowhide drape was drawn back to allow him to enter the birthing chamber and he was greeted by a servant offering him his son to admire. Though there were candles, the light was poor, it was dark now, but Oswald was able to see the child well enough and he thought him something of a wonder to behold. Oswald lightly touched his cheek with the back of his finger, the babe trembled and Oswald smiled. He gazed at the babe sleeping in her arms tightly bound in swaddling so he resembled a little parcelled-up moth in his chrysalis. His eyes were closed and his tiny eyelashes glittered as if sprinkled with gold as the glow of the candlelight brushed over them. There were the most delicate violet shadows beneath them and his skin had the pale bloom of lavender. His breathing was so soft that Oswald could barely hear it, confined as he was within the layers of wrapping.

He knew that many children did not survive infancy. Only the strong survived into adulthood, the struggle of living had begun this day for his son, he laid his fingers lightly on his yet bloody head, and prayed that God might keep him and bless him.

Oswald turned to the bed, and the servant curtseyed, saying, 'my Lady is very tired Lord.'

'Hmm, no doubt,' Oswald went to Helen, knelt and took her hand. Her eyes flickered and she smiled, he leant forward and kissed her lips, they were dry and rough.

'He is beautiful; we will call him *Æthelwald* the name means masculine and ambitious, leader, that's what I want for our son. I want him to be ambitious, not to be resigned to things the way they are, a man who can change things for the better, a man who inspires and a man whom men will follow.

Helen smiled weakly, 'Like his father,' she whispered.

'More like his mother, I hope. I know myself and I would not wish my son to have my shortcomings. How do you feel now my brave wife?'

'Tired, happy, more than that I can't say, I have never been a mother before. I'm glad to have given you a son for our first born, *Æthelwald*, a fine name.'

'Yes, you have made me a proud man, but you must rest, I will be near at hand, never fear, we'll have a life time to talk,' and he reached once more to her, kissed her and left.

229

He'd been several times to see her through the night, but he didn't disturb her, she was sleeping.

When he went at first light, she seemed disturbed, she was sweating; there were beads of sweat standing on her forehead.

'Help me Oswald, I'm so hot, bathe my face.'

'WATER,' he called out, 'COLD WATER.'

A servant entered with a bowl and cloth. Oswald took the cloth from her and dipped it in the water while she held the bowl. He drew back the bedcovers, but he instantly recognised the putrid smell.

'Dear God in heaven, get the Cunning woman, quickly girl.' The girl ran out and he continued to bathe Helen with the cool water, he didn't know what else to do. He knew that this was serious, Helen was writhing and twisting now, she was rapidly becoming delirious; she could no longer hear him.

It only took moments before the girl returned with the Cunning woman, *and* the priest.

The old woman who'd seen it all before said it was the birth flux, and there was naught she could do only wait, keep her warm and pray for the fever to break quickly.

'This day will tell you the will of God, Lord,' was her best miserable offering, as if the God he knew would want this.

The old priest, Father Adam, anointed Helen with oil and prayed for her, but such was her agitation she knocked the small flask of holy oil from his hand. Oswald tried to grab it, but it splashed all over him and ran through his fingers.

'Don't worry about that Lord, I will leave you now, go to the church and pray for her, and you.'

'Aye, aye, pray for us all, the child too. Will you baptise him now Father?'

'Yes, I will attend to that, tell me what is he to be called?'

'Æthelwald.'

In the evening Helen stilled, she seemed at peace after all her striving. Oswald held her in his arms hardly able to hear her above the sound of the pulse pounding in his head... *her* breathing was shallow. Finally, she gave a long – soft – sigh, it was almost, a sigh of relief, and her face relaxed.

Oswald couldn't quite comprehend the moment, how could this be? What had happened? How could she be here, then not here? All he could do was stare at this person who held his heart in her hands, none of this made any sense, this surely couldn't be the end...

'I mean Lord Jesus, I love her, she can't, *not* be here. She's part of me, it can't be; it just can't. How can I live without hearing her laughter, seeing her smile, not for a day, a week, a year, but never, ever again?'

He was squeezing and kissing her hand and pressing his lips to it, tears streamed silently down his face onto her fingers. A hand touched his shoulder and Æbbe knelt down by his side, she was in tears too.

'I'm so sorry, Swald.'

He shook his head in disbelief; he was unable to speak. Never in all his life had he known pain the like of this, he was even struggling to breathe.

Eventually his heart spoke. 'Never again, never again, never again.'

Æbbe didn't know what he meant, it was the sound of some darkness from within, but there was a tragic finality in the moment which was hell on earth for all those who loved another, as Oswald, her Oswald, had loved this woman.

How could a human being recover from such invisible pain as this? No salve other than God's peace could bring relief, true relief that is. Time alone would not heal this, deaden it, hide it perhaps, but heal it, no.

She would be here for her beloved brother, she would pray when he could not, and she would love him when he could not love.

People did not like Oswald they loved him, and Oswiu knew that, he was such a man that had cared for others and they now cared for him. It was unusual for a warrior, to show weakness and vulnerability not the obvious qualities of a hardened man of war, but with Oswald his weakness, his humanness seemed to be his strength.

Poor Eanfrith had to undertake greater and greater heroic deeds for men to take any heed of him, whilst Oswald showed weakness and men would die for him. It was such a contradiction of all that made sense to normal human thought.

God ministered to Oswald through his friends, none more than Oswiu and Æbbe. Æbbe in particular seemed to have the measure of his needs. She understood when to speak, when to hold him and when to stand back. Perhaps it came from the heart of her love, whatever was to be the truth, she was one of those people who understood the deep, unseen needs of others, as if she had special sight.

He sat on his hunkers holding his son to his breast, watching her feeding the chickens, with grain and kitchen scraps from a basket under her arm. He was sure she'd chosen the right path; to give her life completely to God would be the only way for her. It was who she was, and who she would be, for the rest of her life. [28]

'God bless you my dearest sister...' he spoke softly into the hair of his son.

Æbbe told Oswald that Helen had merely left the land of the dying for the land of the living. He remembered Helen saying, on their wedding day – "If heaven is better than this moment, it must be a glorious place indeed".

Wherever heaven was he knew she would be there, and he thanked God for allowing him a brief moment in eternity with such a beautiful person. How blessed was he amongst men.

Chapter 20

News from Bernicia

Oswald was seated with his back against the wattle and daub wall of his roundhouse. He shuffled slightly trying to find a comfortable spot where there was not a hardened stalk sticking annoyingly into his back. It was a warm sunny day, and perhaps after the long endless wet winter this would be a summer to remember. However, in truth, Oswald had too many dates to remember and the balance was now weighing down on the side of the dates that he would rather forget. He thought it odd, as he read his book; that a man's life, with all its trials and heartaches, in the end, amounted to no more than a list of dates. Would that be the sum total of his legacy to his son Æthelwald, he wondered.

He was struggling to concentrate on the text he was reading, he felt sleepy with the heat of the day. Abbot Ségéne had loan him a book on the lives of the holy men of old; it was rare and very costly. He knew how privileged he was to have been trusted with this holy book. It was an open display of the high regard in which he was held by the Abbot, who had been his special friend since he first set foot on Iona.

Oswald thought for a moment, was that in 617. He wasn't quite sure of the date; it seemed like a lifetime ago. He smiled in the light of his thoughts; his life was already assembling its dates. Abbot Ségéne had once said that time, was no more than us passing through eternity.

Oswald had been many times to see Abbot Ségéne, especially since Helen had died. He was ever encouraging when Oswald was in deep despair. Often his life without Helen became too much for him; it was a little better now. The times between the dark days of hell were longer, but no matter how he tried, the pain of losing her would forever catch him when he least expected it, and it could literally bring him to his knees. It was an actual physical thing, as if a knife was stabbing into his heart; the pain was so intense he would sometimes find himself having to hang on to a post, or a wall, to prevent collapsing into a heap, and he would have to pant to regain some control of his breathing. These were the worst of days when hope was lost to him, and he could see no future, then he'd remember the Abbot saying that he'd seen a sign above his head saying, "There is something in your future worth living for".

Oswald glanced up from his book at his future for now, his son, Æthelwald. He was a mixed blessing, if the truth were known, "Wald" as Æbbe insisted on calling him. Oswald smiled; Æbbe had clipped the names of the people she loved, for as long as he could remember. She only came home very occasionally, now that she was at the Abbey. He missed her – and he though how true it was that we take people for granted when they are with us. She had the unerring ability to make complicated things seem simple, ever sensitive to the *real* needs of others. Not our *wants*, which we often wear on the outside – but our needs – not so easily seen.

Æthelwald was nearly two, and was forever doing something he should not be doing. He demanded fulltime attention in this world of fascinating things to touch. Princess Edlin, had taken on the day-to-day care of him, and Eanfrith seemed happy for her to do that. Eanfrith and Edlin had only the one child, their son Talorcan, who was six now. Even at this moment as Oswald watched him, Æthelwald was tormenting a new kitten which seemed to have made Oswald's roundhouse its home and was content to endure Oswald's continuing presence.

Yes, Æthelwald was a mixed blessing, for he was the image of his mother. Sometimes that was a great comfort insomuch that through him he felt as if Helen was yet in reaching distance, just behind a veil, her smiling eyes looking out at him from their son's. On another day to see Æthelwald's beautiful face, was a torturous memory of things lost.

Abbot Ségéne had said to him once that the pain he was suffering was all part of the love he'd had then. The pain now was a measure of their love, both extremes of being human.

Hrodulf had called Æthelwald's cat Cedric, he said his hair was the same nondescript untidy mess that Cedric's always was and the name had stuck.

Suddenly Oswald's contemplations were broken when Æthelwald shrieked, and flopped down onto his bottom holding his bloody finger in the air. Clearly, Cedric had tired of the game and needed to establish who was in command. Cedric had found a position of calm, after his initial shock when Æthelwald shouted, and was now sat on a nearby post licking his paw and attending to his ruffled appearance.

'Lord,' a voice called, Oswald turned as he bent down to pick up Æthelwald and saw a servant running towards him. 'The King wishes to see you; he has had important news. I am to fetch Lord Eanfrith and Lord Oswiu too.'

'And where is the King?'

'He was at the hightable in the longhouse, when he bade me find you, Lord.'

Oswald called to a servant and told her to watch and care for Æthelwald until he returned.

Oswald saw King Domnall Brecc standing at the entrance to the longhouse waiting for him and looking like Cedric when he had his tongue in a bowl of cream.

'Oswald, have you seen Eanfrith?'

'No, I came straight here.'

'I have just received news that your nemesis King Edwin has been killed by King Cadwallon ap Cadfan of Gwynedd. I was told he is now ravaging the land. It appears that his tyranny knows no bounds.'

Oswald was speechless, his uncle dead, he couldn't believe it. He'd never expected this; he was totally unprepared. He had yet to make a comment when Oswiu and Eanfrith came. In contrast to Oswald, Eanfrith needed no time to consider what this might mean. His immediate thought was that they must go now with an army and claim back his birthright.

'One moment, we need much more information before we rush off and risk ending up with the same disaster we were part of last time.'

Eanfrith looked crestfallen at Oswald's less than enthusiastic response.

'Of course Brother, we will need to plan carefully, but it is good news nevertheless, is it not?'

'On the face of it, it sounds very encouraging, but this might be our last chance, therefore we need to be sure that we approach this wisely with understanding and a plan. I am assuming that you will allow me to lead the men as I offered sometime since.' Oswald wanted Eanfrith to be in no doubt where he stood.

'Indeed, you have the greatest number of followers, it would be only sensible for you to lead in any battle.'

'*And I* have not forgotten my oath to you Lord Oswald; I promised you support and I meant it,' King Domnall Brecc added.

'That is very generous Lord. Who brought the news?'

'The fellow is inside I have seen that he has mete and drink. He'd ridden hard, spreading the news so *we* might be prepared in case we in the north are attacked next. This King of Gwynedd wishes to be King of the whole of Briton, so it is said of him.'

'First, with your permission, Lord, I will speak with this rider and find out exactly what he knows.' Oswald turned to Eanfrith, 'Perhaps brother you might rally together our Bernicians and tell them the good tidings, while I talk to this messenger.'

Oswald didn't want Eanfrith confusing the man with his overbearing excitement. 'You come with me Oswiu,' Oswald said quietly tugging at Oswiu's sleeve.

Oswald spent some time making sense of all that the messenger had to say, until he was clear in his mind what the situation was really like in Bernicia.

When he'd first seen the messenger, he was surprised to see a monk, who'd apparently been travelling in Bernicia, spreading the message of the Christian faith, when the death of King Edwin was made known to him.

'And what should I call you brother?'

'I am known as Brother Edgar, I take it that you are the famed Whiteblade.'

Oswald laughed, 'I think that is really my sword, Dream World, you speak of, but some call me that, it's true.'

'Your fame has spread throughout the north, Lord.'

'That may well be so, but it's you who are of interest here, tell me what you know.'

The monk told his tale in greater depth than he had to King Domnall Brecc, for

Oswald was familiar with the names of the people and places in Bernicia, so he had a greater grasp of what was said. It appeared that this King Cadwallon ap Cadfan of Gwynedd, with his fearsome reputation was not occupying Bebbanburg, but merely ravaging the north.

As Oswald listened, he began to think that this really could be an opportunity to retake Bernicia. If the people were suffering under this tyrant, surely they would be ready to join a force led by their own people, sons of the great King Æthelfrith.

Yes! This could be the God given opportunity they'd been waiting for, to return to their home, Bernicia, this was a chance to grasp it with both hands.

Oswald swore that he would lead this invasion, no matter what Eanfrith said. He knew Eanfrith could never do it. Oswald would be content to allow Eanfrith to be the figurehead. He was sure that Eanfrith would be happy with that, and he was certain that *he* would forever have Oswiu's support.

King Domnall Brecc was as good as his word, he gave funds and men; those added to Oswald's own followers made for a

243

formidable force. Even yet Oswald was not about to rush south he insisted that his army trained and practised, at first there were mutterings. This was not the way of warriors, but such was Oswald's charisma that they submitted to his will.

The time to march came, they would take Bebbanburg, it would be their heart, and from there, they would drive out King Cadwallon ap Cadfan of Gwynedd from the whole of Bernicia and reclaim their homeland.

Oswald rose early, as was his practise and went to Helen's grave. He took a small bunch of forget-me-nots with their delicate blue flowers, laid them reverently on the small mound and sat down cross-legged staring at her name on the stone marker. It was an ornate cross, exactly as he had wanted. The stone had been intricately carved by the mason with well worked familiar Saxon patterns of knots and snakes, enforcing their never ending theme, reflecting both Oswald's and God's eternal love.

Yet there were tears, it would be so difficult for him to leave her here when he was in Bernicia, perhaps one day he would have to leave her for good and he didn't know how he would do that. Never to be this close again, it was a hellish thought and he leaned forward on his clenched fists and tried to calm the torment. There were moments of panic when his memory of her face became faint as if behind a veil, these were moments of great anxiety, but the moment would pass and he would find his peace once more. He still couldn't believe she had gone and lifted his eyes heavenward as if hoping for one more glimpse, he would take that, just one glimpse, but it seemed that it was not God's way. Then he lowered his head sadly and prayed.

Hrodulf saw Oswald coming down the slope; he knew where he'd been, as did Oswiu and Daffyd their new comrade and friend.

'*Lord,*' was all Hrodulf said bowing and squeezed his shoulder as he came to his side. 'We are all ready – this day will see men place their foot on the road to victory, I know it Lord, I feel it in my blood.'

'If it is God's will, it will be so Hrodulf, in Him I trust and though a host encamp against me we will not be overcome.'

'That's sounds good to me, Lord. I will take that from any god, even the Christian God.'

Oswald laughed and slapped Hrodulf's back.

'No wonder you and Cedric were such friends you were one and the same.' Oswald glanced at Edlin with Æthelwald in her arms and went to her. Æthelwald reached for him and he took his son from her, lifting him high in the air. Æthelwald giggled. Oswald lowered him gradually until their noses touched, kissed him and returned him into the arms of Edlin. 'Take care of him, my dearest sister Edlin, be sure to tell him all about his mother.'

'I will, and his father too.'

'Aye, and his father, but it is my hope that I will see him again,' he smiled and kissed Edlin.

Oswald was the last to mount; Eanfrith was in high spirits as he led the army away from the fortress of Dunadd, southeast to Bebbanburg and their home of Bernicia.

Brother Edgar would ride south with them and Oswald was glad of his company. They were much of an age; he had been for a time on Iona, so he knew many of the people whom Oswald was familiar with, which bonded Oswiu and Oswald to him.

As they neared the borders of Bernicia there were many signs of raiding, houses burned, animals and humans slaughtered, grim sights for the warriors. Oswald hoped and prayed that he could contain them as their anger grew. He had to trust that the discipline he had attempted to instil within them would hold fast when they met with King Cadwallon's men, which they would sooner or later.

Oswald spent much of the journey talking with Eanfrith; the nearer they got to Bernicia the more Oswald could see the old Eanfrith emerging. He said he would restore the old gods to their place of honour and with them the greatness of Bernicia as it was in his father's day. If Eanfrith noticed the despair in Oswald's eyes, he chose to ignore it. He was not going to be dissuaded from his restoration plans by Oswald, but Oswald knew that Eanfrith only saw life through the narrow vision of his *wants* and could not cope with that larger picture, which may present a more unfavourable view, bringing with it a challenge to his vision.

Oswald was quite at a loss, he didn't try to challenge Eanfrith, as it seemed he had not learned anything from their previous venture to Bernicia. Eanfrith would never be able to hold onto this kingdom no matter how he wished for it.

There was much unknown before them, but Oswald feared *most* the foolishness of his brother. He talked with Oswiu, but neither could settle in their minds Eanfrith's total lack of understanding or leadership, yet their leader, he was determined to be.

The fortress was in view now as the army stopped in more or less the same place as it had when they last came to challenge King Edwin. Oswald leant forward onto the up-stand of his saddle, and eased his backside from his seat, it was hot and sore, he needed to dismount and stretch his legs while he took in the vista before him.

'We will dismount and spend the night here. We all need to gather our thoughts and be refreshed. From now on we will be in constant danger.'

'I'm not sure about this Oswald, we should strike whilst the iron is hot.'

Oswald paused, straightened himself, and looked Eanfrith in the eye. 'Eanfrith, I was not offering a suggestion that we might stay here for the night, for your approval, let me make it quite clear, *this* is what we are going to do.'

Eanfrith visibly drew back, clearly shaken by the force of Oswald's declaration. From this point on, if there *had* been some doubt before, there must be *no* doubt now, Oswald was in command, and Eanfrith was not. Even if he were *King* Eanfrith, what was to happen in the days ahead, would only happen on Oswald's yea or nay.

Oswald walked to the edge of the camp with Oswiu and they stared into the distance.

'We are here once more Oswald, I doubted that we ever would be.'

'Yes, I wondered too, many times, but as you say, we are here and I am not leaving, but that we are the victors. I will, by the grace of God have Bernicia returned to our Leodwalding family. This is where my son Æthelwald, will grow up. I will extinguish those fires of burning lives and homes that we see in the distance, and light a fire for God which will *never* be extinguished.'

Oswald left the last task of the night to Oswiu, which was to see that guards were in place and the list of changes and times had been made clear to those guarding the camp.

Chapter 21

The King is Dead

Oswald sat for sometime on his mount staring at the fortress, no one said a word to him. Oswiu watched him out of the corner of his eye, he dare do no more; Oswald never blinked. The only movement to be seen was the rhythmic flexing of his jaw muscles. Even his horse stood statuesque, apart from the occasionally flicking of its ears.

'So God, it has come to this, the gates of the city of our birthright are before us. We are come as an army to claim it back, but what of the people inside, our people, do they not have a right to expect their king to protect rather than destroy them? Eanfirth desires to enter his kingship on the tails of a great battle – but what would be his legacy? Show me the right of it all God.'

There was a moment when Oswiu thought that Eanfrith was going to speak to Oswald, but he must have thought better of it.

The whole army waited for his instruction; finally, he tugged on the rein and turned to face his warriors.

'I will ride up to the gate of the fort and speak to their leader.'

'Lord!' Hrodulf pushed his pony forward, 'that's too dangerous, let *me* go, I will tell them whatever it is you want to say.'

Oswald looked at him and formed a soft smile on his lips. 'No, I thank you for your concern my friend, but I will do it,' and he turned his mount, trotted along the beach and up to the gates of the fortress and stopped.

All Oswiu could hear was the surf tumbling up the beach and rolling back again dragging the soft sand with it. Horses and men were standing in total silence.

'I am Prince Oswald of Bernicia, son of the great King Æthelfrith, a fair and generous Lord.' Oswald called up to the guards, 'who ruled and lived in this fortress. Now you Bernicians, whom he loved, cared and died for, close your gates to his sons. We are the rightful heirs of his kingdom, and we have travelled far to free you noble people of Bernicia from a tyrant and oppressor, not to enslave you, and this is how you treat us, you shame us. Fear not, we will not molest you our brothers, instead we will return from whence we came in great sadness.'

'Prince Oswald, is that really you?' A voice called from the ramparts.

'I am Prince Oswald, who is this, who addresses me?'

'I am Ælfweard, the friend of Cedric, do you remember me? I was ill when you left with your mother the Queen those many years since and could not go with you. I thought that I was dying, don't you remember? You came to me and wished me well.'

'I remember an Ælfweard,' now it was Oswald's turn to look surprised. 'If you are whom you say, why are these gates barred?'

'We fear Cadwallon ap Cadfan, he is destroying Bernicia, though he has not tried to attack us yet, we are ready.' Ælfweard

252

disappeared from view, a shout was heard and the heavy oak gates began to slowly swing open. Oswald narrowed his eyes when he saw this old man standing before him, bowing.

Oswald walked his horse forward to the man and the man stood up.

'Ælfweard, it is you!' Oswald said leaping from his horse and embracing him. 'How I rejoice to see you my old friend, I thought you long departed from this life. Praise be to God, this is a great blessing indeed to find old friends here in Bebbanburg, now I know I am truly home.'

'Do you remember Godric?' Ælfweard swept his hand towards Godric standing nearby.

'Of course I do, you look well Godric.'

'We are the only two boyhood friends left now, once there were five of us. We two, Cedric and Wulfstan, who you never knew, he was the greatest of us. If I'm not mistaken that is his sword you now wear.' Ælfweard said twisting his head to better see Oswald's sword, 'a gift from Cedric I dare say, you must be a great warrior Lord, for Cedric to give you that holy sword.'

'You said there were five of you!'

'Aye, so I did, sadly there was Lord Wulfstan's traitorous brother, who we never speaks of, forgive me Lord I can't bring

253

myself to utter his name.' There was a moment of tense silence until Oswald spoke.

'I will call the others,' Oswald walked back outside the gate and beckoned Eanfrith, Oswiu and Hrodulf to join him.

They hesitated, looked at each other then rode forward up the bank and into the fortress.

Once they had nervously dismounted, Oswald introduced Eanfrith to the fort defenders, though most there already knew him.

'This is your new king,' and the defenders dutifully bowed, but Oswald wondered if Eanfrith would be truly accepted.

He knew that it was important that any claimant to the throne as rightful heir, in the Saxon world, should have been born while their father was king.

Unfortunately, Eanfrith was born before Æthelfrith was the king; he was born whilst King Hussa was on the Bernician throne. Even if he had been born when Æthelfrith was on the throne, he would yet need the final approval of the Witan before he'd be accepted.

For now, it appeared as if those here in the fort, were simply relieved, and prepared to see them as a gift of hope, when there seemed to be no hope. Oswald could understand that they would initially accept Eanfrith; time might have a different story to tell, much would depend on how Eanfrith acted. However, there would be an initial period of grace.

Over the next months, King Cadwallon ap Cadfan of Gwynedd continued his raiding. Oswald had tried to engage Cadwallon's forces, but he had never been successful they had always managed to evade his efforts to confront them.

The chase had led Oswald to the northwest, Cear Luel [29] where the old Roman Wall ended. He was seated at the table in his tent writing when he received the stunning blow. Godric, old as he was, had ridden through the night to bring him the news. Godric had been given the task because Oswald knew him of old, and the nature of this message must not carry with it any shadow of doubt. Godric came into the tent with Hrodulf and bowed. Oswald pointed to a chair, he could see that Godric was exhausted; Godric bowed once more and sighed as he sat down.

'Bring refreshment for this warrior.'

255

'Thank you Lord.'

'Now, then Godric, what brings you all the way from Bebbanburg, not a ride for a man of your years?'

'Bad news Lord.'

Oswald didn't answer; he lay back in his chair and gestured with open palms for Godric to speak.

'King Eanfrith... has been murdered by King Cadwallon.' Oswald's sat up straight in his chair; his face was as stone.

'Go on,' Oswald's spoke without emotion, steady and measured.

'Cadwallon summoned King Eanfrith to the Roman town of Corbridge, on the northern edge of our Bernician kingdom, under a flag of truce. Eanfrith went with a twelve-man guard of warriors, treasure and hostages as is customary, under the assumption that Cadwallon wanted to negotiate some sort of peace settlement. We were told that Cadwallon had them decapitated and their heads displayed on spiked posts.'

Throughout this distressing report, Oswald yet never moved, apart from clenching his fists so tightly his hands were white. He was furious on a number of accounts. One – Eanfrith had made great play of rejecting the Christian faith and restoring the pagan gods to Bernicia. In

Oswald's eyes that made Eanfrith and the whole kingdom vulnerable. This was deeply offensive to Oswald who was a devout Christian. Secondly Oswald could not believe Eanfrith's stupidity, he should never have gone to meet with Cadwallon, never mind with only twelve men. He ought to have known what a foolhardy venture that was, at the very least Eanfrith should have discussed his intention with him before he did anything. This madness could well result in a victory for Cadwallon, for who else had the ability and resources to defeat Cadwallon, but them. Such thoughts must have been predominant when he contemplated this flagrant demonstration of his contempt for traditions of battlefield conduct. The man was without honour in any shape or form, he was no more than a thief and a brigand.

Oswald decided that his army would follow the Roman wall across country to Corbridge, where his spies told him Cadwallon and his forces were camped. It would be three days of strenuous travel before they fought the battle, but Oswald was certain he would not make the same mistake as King Conadd Cerr made in Hibernia, when they were brutally defeated at Fid Eóin. No – once they set off, they would not be camping overnight to give Cadwallon time to prepare his defences, where Oswald stopped would be the place to do battle.

Oswald would expect support from Royth, son of Rhun who had also been tormented by Cadwallon.

Oswald had demonstrated great political foresight, when he'd arranged the betrothal of his brother Oswiu to Princess Rhieinmelth, the daughter of Royth. He had not long been betrothed, but that union brought with it forces from the north east, and the fine horses they now sat upon, which had been a gift from Royth, son of Rhun.

Oswald gave an impassioned speech at the betrothal of the two, to ensure Royth's support when the defining battle came, as he was sure it would.

'Will the warriors of Rheged stand by their allies against the perfidious apostate, Cadwallon, who like a cursed whelp seeks only to destroy the north parts of our island with rapine and slaughter. Will the King cement our friendship in the name of the True God by honouring the betrothal in Christ, of our brother Oswiu to his

258

daughter Rhieinmelth, agreed upon in the time of our fathers.'

Arranging the betrothal of Oswiu was not difficult, for he was a Prince of Bernicia and as such, a person of great consequence. It was said of him that he was tall and handsome, pleasant of speech, courteous of manner to both commoner and nobleman alike, and loved by all because of his great dignity.

Although Oswiu had already fathered a child with a beautiful Hibernian Princess, called Fina, it was not seen as any hindrance to the advantages of being betrothed to a Leodwalding atheling.

Oswald had become a formidable leader, and was now, since the murder of his brother Eanfrith, the King of Bernicia in all but name. His fame as a fearless warrior had spread throughout the north. Adding the gilding to his fame was his overwhelming charisma, known integrity, and political understanding, which made him both an implacable friend and enemy.

To some, the connection between the legendary Hibernian god, Nuada Airgetlám, who'd lost an arm in battle, which was then replaced by a silver arm – and the similarities of Oswald's name of Whiteblade or "Whitearm", was not missed. It was also said that when his beloved wife,

Princess Helen, was on her death bed, she'd poured holy oil over his right arm.

Oswald knew his friend Abbot Ségéne, never missed an opportunity to add mystique and weight to his protégé's story. He had once told Oswald that the Church could be a powerful ally. He had not fully understood at the time, what the Abbot had meant, but he did now. The Abbot said that he should be content to allow the stories to be told; it was all in God's hands. Oswald was not totally at peace with this thought, but it seemed it was beyond his control. Not only was he now seen as a warrior and a king in waiting, but also a holy man, and an anointed servant of the Living God.

Travelling near the great wall made the journey quick and relatively easy. The route had been maintained as a way of travelling across country by traders, shepherds and drovers alike since the Romans left, some said more than four lifetimes past.

The mid-summer rivers yet ran with ale coloured water draining off the high moors. At Greenhead's narrow pass, Oswald sent scouts ahead of his force for it was the ideal place for an ambush. However, their spies returned informing them that there was no such ambush waiting for them. It seemed that Cadwallon was blissfully unaware of Oswald's oncoming force.

Oswald was greatly encouraged from the reports that Cadwallon seemed oblivious to his presence, for he was sure that his army would have been seen by now. He concluded, that it could only mean that the local people knew of him and wholly supported him.

Oswald picked his spot for the fight, he was sure that God was with him. The battle would take place at Hefenfelth [30] they made that their camp for the night and set about preparing for the morrow's battle.

While Oswald slept that night in his tent, he had a dream, he dreamt of Colm Cille [31] a man he'd never known. The Saint shone with angelic beauty, he was so tall his head seemed to touch the clouds and as he stood in their camp, he covered it all but for one corner with his shining robe. Colm Cille spoke to Oswald in the dream just as God had spoken to Joshua, saying:

'Be strong and act manfully, behold I will be with you.' The saint also said, *'This night go out from your camp for the Lord has granted you that your foes shall be put to flight and Cadwallon, your enemy shall be delivered into your hands and you shall return victorious after the battle, and reign happily.'*

Oswald awoke trembling; he was sweating. He wiped the back of his hand

261

across his forehead to clear the sweat from his eyes. He'd never had a dream that was so stunningly clear, as the one he'd been awoken by; he was in a state of utter bewilderment. There was an earthenware jug of cold water by his cot and he filled a bowl and washed, but the dream would not leave him it was so vivid he felt that he could have reached out and touched Saint Colm Cille.

Oswald awoke his leaders to tell them of his dream. The sleepy confused men Christian and pagan alike, were to a man touched by the telling of Oswald's vision and felt the powerful encouragement it engendered.

'You must tell the men of this Lord; it will bring great encouragement. We are all men the same. When the hour of the battle draws near, fear and doubt touches every man. Believe me Lord, I am too old, and have been here too many times, not to know the truth of it.'

At first light, Oswald repeated the tale of his dream and the men listened intently. As he spoke aloud the words of Saint Colm Cille, *'Your enemy shall be delivered into your hands and you shall return victorious after the battle,'* he felt with deep conviction that his life as a warrior was pleasing to God. He did not need to fear

262

that the manner of his birth was a hindrance to God, for had he not said through the Saint he would reign?

So powerfully did Oswald feel God's blessing that he had men erect a wooden cross on the site so that all might see that they, these Bernician warriors, fought for the Living God, his God, and his priests blessed the cross and prayed for the warriors.

After the priests had blessed the cross, the warriors launched their attack on the camp of Cadwallon, near Hagustaldesham [32] Oswald's warriors achieved almost total surprise. The Britons were forced to run, with the Bernicians in hot pursuit, the Britons were eventually trapped and massacred, along with Cadwallon himself, and his most faithful warriors who'd surrounded him at a place called Divelis. [33]

Oswald thought that they had probably hoped to cross the river and escape onto the moors. Even though Oswald's force was smaller than the Briton's, they had overwhelmed them, the defeat was total, there was no mercy shown, their bodies were left to rot in the bloody river where they'd been killed. This was a great victory by any standards and Oswald knew it would be talked about for many years.

After the battle, Oswald knelt in his tent and gave thanks to God for His kindness to the Bernician people.

Chapter 22

A New Friend

Oswald was now the King of Bernicia; he'd been crowned at Caer Urfa [34] at the eastern end of the great Roman Wall. It had been a windy day at the end of Winterfilleð [35] when he had been proclaimed King of Bernicia on a hilltop called Lawe Top, some now called the hill, *Oswald's* Hill, in memory of the great occasion.

265

He had wanted to return to his capital of Bebbanburg as their undisputed King, the son of the *great* King Æthelfrith of Bernicia and confirmed as his rightful heir by the Elders of the Witan.

Oswald felt to be a man chosen by God; he had never sought any of this. Abbot Ségéne told him that the Christ was called the son of David, but he was not in fact the descendant of the great King David. He was *God's* son, conceived of the Holy Ghost.

The Christ had taken on David's name from his adopted father's line. Oswald felt his lineage was in some way similar, because his father was not actually King Æthelfrith. His father was the Lord Wulfstan who was exalted by all who knew him and his mother was Queen Aefre, but he, Oswald was known by all as the son of Æthelfrith and always had been.

The names of his mother and father, and their love, forever touched Oswald's heart, they, their names, and their sacrifice would be forgotten. The little he knew of their story was that two people had loved enough to lay down their lives. They had done no more than that, they had not wanted such a love; they'd tried to run from it. Unlike the Christ, Oswald reflected, they, their names, and their sacrifice would be forgotten.

Cedric had told him that he set no one above his father Wulfstan, that his honour, goodness and kindness was an example to all, this had been the testimony of all those who'd ever known him. God in His goodness had seen fit to have mercy upon them and *he* had been blessed because of them. As with David and Bathsheba, God had seen fit to give them a son and make him the great King Solomon, famed for his wisdom and wealth. So also had God made him, Oswald of Bernicia son of Wulfstan and Aefre, a King, and he would serve God as long as he lived. He, by the grace of the Living God, would bring Christianity to all he ruled; his would be a Godly kingdom, a light in the pagan darkness of Briton.

Oswald sat at his work table tapping the soft feathered end of his quill on his lip, contemplating the events of his history that had brought him thus far, some times of great joy, but there were other's of yet unbearable sorrow. The pain of losing his beloved Helen ever tormented his heart. He looked around the room, it was incomplete as would every place be, wherever he set foot, or laid his head at the end of a day.

'Dear God, how lonely I am, forgive me.' A quiet voice in his head reminded him of a piece of scripture from the prophet Joel, *"I will restore to you the years that the locusts have eaten".*

Suddenly, there was a scratching of the end of his long worktable and he turned his head to the sound, it took a moment for his tear filled eyes to focus. There was a large black bird, a Raven, pecking contentedly at a plate of half eaten food, which had not yet been cleared away by his servant.

It was the strangest thing, and then he remembered how in the scripture story God had sent ravens to minister to Elijah when he was distressed. Was this God's way of speaking to him and telling him He knew of his need and He would feed him?

Oswald was in this moment lifted from his despair and gave thanks. The bird looked at him as if it might speak, cocking its head first to one side, and then to the other. Oswald gently set down his quill, and slowly reached out his hand to the glossy black bird, but it was startled and flapped its wings then it settled once more and came to him laying its beak in the palm of his hand. He gently touched the tip of his finger to the crown of its head and the creature seemed perfectly content. He smiled, for he was sure that he'd made a friend this day.

He decide in that moment that he would write to his friend, Abbot Ségéne and ask his advice about how best to further the

268

gospel of the Christ God in his kingdom. He remembered that they had talked about the island of Lindis Feorna or Metcaud, as the Abbot called it. Perhaps the wily old fox always had such a plan in mind Oswald thought, pausing and smiling. In any event, Oswald knew that his friend would be able to advise him.

Oswald had heard that his uncle King Edwin had tried, even if it was half heartedly, to set up some Christian work. Alas, the Bishop named Paulinus from Deira who had been set the task, had only limited successes, and had fled south after Edwin had been killed. It had been said of the Bishop, that his manner was one, which did not please the Bernicians, but Oswald did not know the truth of that.

No one seemed to know where the fellow was now.

While Oswald waited for the reply from Abbot Ségéne he decide to travel round his kingdom and also to those minor kingdoms of which he was Overlord, such as the kingdom of the West Saxons.

Oswald had heard that there was a Christian work being done, with some success, in the royal house of Gewisse and he wanted to encourage and lend his support to it.

He'd been told by Abbot Ségéne that a bishop called Birinus had been sent from Rome. His original commission entailed preaching to parts of Briton where no missionary efforts had reached, and it may have included instructions to reach the Mercians in particular. However, at this time, he had gone no further than the West Saxon kingdom of King Cynegils.

King Cynegils seemed content to allow Bishop Birinus to preach the faith of the Christ God to the people of the West Saxons.

It was also rumoured that King Cynegils wanted the support of the new king of Bernicia to help him secure his kingdom against the Mercians, clearly Oswald's fame as a holy warrior king, was spreading throughout Briton.

'Yes!' Oswald decided, as he sat at his table with his new friend, that was where he would make his first visit, and then he would wend his way slowly up country back to his home, visiting the people of his new kingdom and establishing his rule. It had been a long road to this place in his life, but he believed that God's timing was always perfect. He'd had much to learn and when he looked back over the way he'd travelled, he could clearly see the hand of God.

If King Edwin had not forced them to flee from Bernicia, he knew that he'd never have gone to Iona. That he'd never have met Abbot Ségéne, never learned how to read and write, never learned the art of warfare, at the expense of other kings, never found the most Holy God, and he'd never have discovered how *He* could hold and support a human being through even the blackest torments of life.

He'd found a God who'd chosen to make His home in the suffering degradation of mankind, so that He could share in man's most desperate moments. A God, who would not turn from the rejection, failings and torments of His creation, a God who had sent his only Son to redeem His wilful and rebellious children. He knew now that his weakness was God's strength, and so when he was weak, and all was against him, God was at His strongest.

'In thee have I trusted, let me never be confounded.'

Oswald was setting off into a new world, and for the first time he would be leaving the old world behind, starkly highlighted by the waving hand of Hrodulf. He could not call on him forever, he was old and this was a long journey, He'd earned the time to be at his ease. When he argued, and he did argue with Oswald, his challenge was not to his King, but to his friend for that's what Oswald was to him. Oswald had learned how to fight; now he needed to learn how to stand and rule. The two had been through so much together, they'd love the same people, Oswald could ask no more and Hrodulf could give no more.

Oswald did however leave Hrodulf with a smile on his face, saying that he now had a greater responsibility than caring for him. He was to care for his new friend, "Theophilus", friend of God, his raven, who followed him everywhere.

Oswald tried to smile at the thought of leaving; thankfully, he still had Oswiu by his side, but he was leaving Æthelwald, his son. His birthday was forever a miserable date to remember, but Oswald loved him and he his father, he was a fine boy. Æthelwald had wanted to come with him, but Oswald felt it was too uncertain to risk his wellbeing, Hrodulf would care for him, Oswald knew that.

He recalled how he'd felt when his father King Æthelfrith had left on similar journeys as the one he was undertaking, but these sacrifices were part of being King and he would accept them as such.

The journey took five days, longer than Oswald thought it would, he was overwhelmed by the reception he received from villages on his way. People were calling him a saint; they'd heard stories of how people had been healed by merely getting close to the wooden cross he'd erected at Hefenfelth, where he'd defeated King Cadwallon and his army.

It was said that one day a horseman was riding near Oswald's cross when his horse began to feel great pain. It rolled in agony on the ground, apparently dying, but at the sight of the cross, it was immediately cured. Its owner told the story at the nearest inn, and the people there decided to take a paralysed girl to the same spot. She was cured too.

It seemed that everyone they met had heard of his vision of Saint Colm Celli and how he'd told Oswald, that the victory against Cadwallon would be his.

Oswald was certain that the majority of people he met would not be followers of the

Christian God, but that did not appear to make the slightest difference. People who were sick pushed towards him hoping for a chance to touch him. Even as he travelled, the stories followed in his wake, of how people had been healed after touching him or his clothing.

Oswald was mightily relieved when he finally dismounted at the court of King Cynegils, but even there, people treated him with a reverence, that such as Abbot Ségéne would not be unfamiliar.

King Cynegils and his family came out of their longhouse to greet him, even Bishop Birinus had come to meet him and he went as far as to kneel before Oswald. Oswald was so confused by this absurd treatment he could only stand in silence smiling like the fool he felt.

'You do us a great honour Lord; we are blessed amongst men that you should come to visit us. The Bishop here tells us that God's hand is upon you and that it is a sign from the true God that I should be baptised.'

'And what do you think, King Cynegils? It is not for me to instruct you, it's you who must decide what God is saying to you, but we are tired from the journey we will talk on this later, might we bathe...' Oswald was distracted from the embarrassment he was feeling when he caught sight of a beautiful young woman smiling at him.

King Cynegils gave orders to servants to tend to the needs of King Oswald and his men and then he turned once more to Oswald and began to introduce his family to him. The beautiful young woman was his daughter, Cyneburh. Oswald could only stare at the woman. She was uncannily like his beloved wife Helen, and this, was almost a repeat of the day when he first arrived at Dunadd, all those years past. It was not until Oswiu tugged at his sleeve that he realised he was yet staring at the woman.

Servants led them to the house where they would be staying and a very fine house it was, Oswald could plainly see how he was to be treated by King Cynegils, for all was done to impress upon him the honour in which he was to be held.

Chapter 23

Cyneburh

Oswald lay down on his cot, with his head resting on his linked hands.

'This has been a strange adventure Oswiu, has it not?'

'Certainly strange for me, I have never known a saint before, let alone touched one...' Oswiu ducked as one of Oswald's gauntlets flew passed his ear and he laughed.

'This is difficult enough for me without your input, brother, pass me my gauntlet and be glad it was not my seax.' Oswald was struggling to turn the last days travelling here into anything approaching a jest.

'I'm sorry, Oswald, but I'm laughing in an attempt to keep myself in some world of reality, while we wend our way through this maze of unravelled lonnens, in which we now find ourselves,' Oswiu said passing the gauntlet back to Oswald.

'I know what you mean, Oswiu, it's beyond anything I've ever heard of.'

Oswiu sat down on his bed, 'I wish Abbot Ségéne was here to ask, perhaps he'd be better equipped to understand all this than we are.'

'Who knows, on another line of thought, what did you make of King Cynegils' daughter, Princess Cyneburh?'

Oswiu narrowed his eyes and looked suspiciously at Oswald who was staring nonchalantly up into the rafters. 'Why do you ask?'

'Oh – no particular reason, Brother, merely making conversation, no more than that... It's strange that she is not wed though, she is surely past the age when she would expect to be wedded, and she has tolerable features.'

'Perhaps no one wanted her,' Oswiu suggested teasingly, whilst tugging off his boot and massaging his toes. He could be obtuse too, if that's Oswald wanted.

There was some activity outside and Oswald lifted his head to see what it was, just as servants carrying a large tub came through the door.

'Lord, your tub...' the fellow said stating the obvious. 'We'll fill it in a minute, Lord, can we gets anything else for thee?' the man said nervously, never lifting his head.

'Not at the moment, we'll bathe first.'

Two servants entered with towels, they obviously had been set the work of bathing them. Whilst several others trundled in and out with large jugs of steaming hot water, Oswald undressed.

Clearly, they were to be bathed and dressed under the supervision of these diligent servants.

'We have more servants here than at home, Lord, and prettier too.' The girl preparing to scrub Oswald smiled at Oswiu's comment.

'Indeed.'

Once they were both bathed, and dressed, they were shown into an attractively decorated hall with the usually painted patterns on the woodwork, and hunting scenes on the walls. They were taken to the hightable and Oswald was given the most elevated seat, which surely was where King Cynegils would normally sit.

He wasn't sure exactly why he was being treated with such excessive deference. Was it because he was their Overlord or because they thought him some great holy man or did King Cynegils merely want to ensure his support against his Mercian enemies?' It was unsettling and he felt uneasy, but then he shrugged, what did it matter anyway.

A servant drew back his chair so that he could take his place at the table then he pushed it carefully under him. Once Oswald was seated, the others there took their places. King Cynegils sat to his right and his wife next to him, beside her their son Cwichelm then Oswiu. On Oswald's left sat the Princess Cyneburh, then Bishop Birinus. She bowed her head respectfully and smiled as she took her seat.

Oswald was slightly amused by the seating arrangements. He was surprised that he was seated next to the Princess, he would have expected to be seated between Prince

Cwichelm and the King, but he knew well Prince Cwichelm's history with Bernicia. He had not travelled all this way, without being well informed about the places and people he was going to encounter. If they took him for a naive saint, they were in for a rude awakening.

He knew fine well that King Cynegils had been concerned about the rise of Bernician power in the north. King Cynegils had ceded the northern half of his kingdom to his son, Cwichelm, effectively creating some protection for his kingdom in the process. He also forged a temporary alliance with the Mercians who were equally concerned about the growing power of the Bernicians, and this alliance was sealed by the marriage of Cynegils' youngest son Cenwalh, who was noticeable by his absence this night, to the sister of King Penda of Mercia.

In 626, the hot-headed Cwichelm launched an unsuccessful assassination attempt on King Edwin of Bernicia. Oswald smiled as he recalled the tale he'd been told. Edwin subsequently sent his army to confront the West Saxons and both sides clashed at a place called Bēamford [36] over to the west of Briton. With the Mercians at their side, the West Saxons had a far larger army than the Bernicians, and went into the battle with complete confidence, but they were defeated due to poor tactics. Oswald had been told that the Bernicians had dug into the side of a place called, "Win Hill" and when the West Saxon forces started moving forward, they were met by a barrage of boulders that had been rolled from the Bernician position above them.

This had been a humiliating defeat for both Cynegils and Cwichelm, and they subsequently retreated within their own borders. The following years saw the Mercians take advantage of the weakened West Saxons by taking the old Roman towns of Gloucester, Bath and Cirencester from them.

The assault today was a more subtle form of attack, and one, to which Oswald was not averse. He for one, was no more likely to object to the attention of a beautiful young woman, than any other man would be, suppose he was a saint. He a saint, 'Ha,' he actually made himself laugh at the absurdity. The Princess frowned, no doubt wondering about his seemingly unwarranted amusement.

Oswald saw her narrow her eyes as she glanced at him. 'Forgive my rudeness Princess; I was merely laughing at myself,

281

and how people apparently see me. I am really such an ordinary fellow.'

'Can a King be so ordinary Lord? Perhaps because you see yourself in such a manner, it makes you anything but ordinary.'

It was now Oswald's turn to be taken aback, but he was not afforded the time to think on what she had said. King Cynegils stood, lifted his drinking cup, banged on the table and the hum of chatter and laughter quickly died.

'Let all who are gathered here, drink to the health and future of the great Warrior and King of Bernicia. We welcome you, King Oswald, all here in this hall and are pleased to share this humble feast with you.'

At which there was raucous banging on the tables and cheering. Oswald did no more than lift his silver cup and dip his head in acknowledgement and respect of the greeting. Once the guests had settled again to their seats, Oswald turned to the Bishop and asked him to bless their mete. A faint smile touched his lips as those who had eagerly began to feast slowly set down the mete they had only just picked up.

The Bishop stood and gave thanks for the mete, bowed to Oswald and took his seat once more.

There was ale for all, but for them fine wine was on offer; the Princess lifted the jug and set it to his cup for his approval.

'Do you wish for wine, Lord?' Clearly, she was serving him as a demonstration of humility to their Overlord.

'You are very kind Princess,' he nodded and she carefully filled his cup. 'Tell me about yourself, Princess.'

'What is it you wish to know Lord?'

'Whatever you wish to tell me, what do you enjoy doing for example?'

She hesitated; Oswald could see she was finding his directness difficult. 'I like riding Lord, I ride most days.'

'That's good, so do I, will you let me join you on the morrow? You can show me your home.'

Her eyes brightened, 'If you wish it, I would be delighted to, Lord.'

'I wish it,' he laughed and she smiled too, showing beautiful even white teeth framed by the most perfect red lips.

As he leaned forward and set his cup to the table, he thought, this was the most honest laughter he'd had since Helen had died.

The following morning Oswald was up bright and early, it was a fine day and he would hold Princess Cyneburh to her promise that she would go riding with him. It would be an ideal opportunity to find out about the West Saxon kingdom and its people.

Oswald was reluctant to admit to himself, never mind his brother Oswiu, that on this particular morning he wanted to know more about Princess Cyneburh than the West Saxons.

Oswald was slightly unsettled as he sat at the table for the breaking of his night's fast. He tried to enter into the conversation with others who had gathered around him. All seemed eager for his company, but he'd hoped to see Princess Cyneburh and as of yet she had not shown her face. Perhaps he had made her feel too uncomfortable at the feast the night past and she wanted to avoid him.

The brightness of his awakening mood was rapidly disappearing into an altogether gloomier, overcast day.

He wondered where Oswiu was, he'd told him that he wanted to see the smith before he came to break his night's fast, but he had not as yet appeared.

As Oswald was leaving the hall, a servant came to him and bowed.

'Yes!'

'The Princess has asked me to make it known to you Lord that she is at the stables if you yet wish to go riding with her.'

Suddenly, Oswald's gloom was dispersed by a ray of sunlight.

'Take me to the Princess.'

When the stables came into view, Oswald could see Princess Cyneburh standing by two fine mounts, dressed for riding. As he approached them both horses snorted and pawed on the floor of the yard, eager to be off.

'My Lord,' she said bowing. 'I hoped that you yet wish to join me.'

Oswald bowed to her, 'Indeed, I assumed that you had either forgotten or were otherwise engaged. However, I'm delighted that was not the case.' Oswald nodded to four warriors and the maid who were clearly there to accompany them.

Oswald mounted, he was known as an accomplished horseman, and he'd been given a fine steed.

As they rode from the fort gates, he glanced at a flock of crows taking flight from a fallow field, and flying ponderously across the smoke streaked blue sky before them. All seemed well with the world this fine morning.

They were clear of the fort and the nearby sleepy village before they spoke. Oswald brought his horse nearer to Cyneburh's and they slowed their pace to a trot. The two horses shook their heads and snorted rattling their harnesses, clearly wanting to press on, not yet ready to walk, but like Oswald, Cyneburh was quite able to establish that she was in command of her mount, not the mount in command of her.

They were now leisurely walking their horses along a riverbank, the words kept running round and around his head, "I will restore to you, I will restore to you", the words that he had on his mind in his room at Bebbanburg before he'd decided to come here. Everything about this meeting reminded him of his first meeting with Helen.

'Are you well Lord, you seem distracted?'

'I am indeed well, my Lady,' he answered, ducking his head under a leafy branch which crossed their path, and that was the truth, he felt more at ease, at peace, complete, than he'd felt for years. He didn't really know what the word was to describe how he was feeling. 'Tell me Princess, how can it be that someone such as you is not wedded? Forgive me if that is too personal a question.'

'I might ask you the same, Lord.'

Oswald nodded his head, 'Indeed you might, Princess.' His happy mood had now been changed by a simple question, his smile now left his face and he stared into the distance. They rode on in silence for some time; all the while, he strummed his fingers nervously on his thigh, wondering what to say. Most avoided asking such a question of him, so he'd never had to say much about his feelings of Helen. It was something too painful to face up to, so he pushed it to one side, he knew he'd never moved on, he clung to her memory, it was all he had. This woman had innocently confronted him and he had not been prepared for the challenge.

'Might we dismount for a while and sit on the riverbank,' he asked, trying to sound perfectly at his ease.

'If it is your wish, Lord.'

Oswald dismounted first then reached up to aid the Princess, she rested her hands on his shoulders and he lowered her to the ground. He laid his cloak on the sward, took her hand and she sat down, he seated himself next to her, drew his knees to his chest and wrapped his arms around his legs.

'Have I offended you, Lord?'

'No, no, forgive me... I – *have* been married – and I have a son of some ten years, ten years,' he repeated. 'Has it really been so long, – my wife...' he bowed his head, 'was called Helen,' he said in a soft voice. 'She died when my son was born. I have never really talked about it before this moment, to my friend, the Abbot of Iona, perhaps, *but* not to anyone else, that seems odd now I mention it.'

'Clearly it was a love match, Lord.'

'Yes – a love match. We'd been in love since we were young, no more than children, I guess,' he gasped and tried to control his speech. 'Aye – we were in love.'

'I was betrothed once, to a Prince from Mercia. The threat from Mercia is ever a concern of my father's, but the man caught some flux or other and died before we were wedded.'

'Now it is I who should ask for your forgiveness, I'm sorry to hear such a thing.'

'No need, I had but met him once, there was no love there. If I may say more,' she smiled and lowered her voice, 'you will see now what a rebellious, traitorous daughter I am, when I make known to you that my father hopes to foist me onto the King of Bernicia.'

'*What, me!*'

'You see – such foolishness.'

'Forgive me, I meant no insult. I would see that to be an honour,' and he smiled at her and touched her hand. From that moment on their talk was easy, this was a long forgotten experience for him. In fact, he could only ever remember really talking to one woman, Helen, and of course his beloved Æbbe.

'Perhaps we should return, I'm not usually gone for such a time.'

'My fault, come Princess, let us ride back, perhaps we will keep our conversation to ourselves, that those concerned may wonder.' She laughed, they both laughed, he stood, reached down to her, took her hand and raised her to her feet.

When they rode into the fort, the first person Oswald saw was Oswiu, who nodded most knowingly at him, much to Oswald's infuriation. Oswald dismounted and lifted Cyneburh from her saddle; she bowed and left, escorted by her maid. Oswald paused, took a deep breath and walked to where his brother was smugly sitting.

'Was that a pleasant ride Brother?'

'Yes, I learned a great deal in casual conversation, things that I would not have learned in a more formal setting.'

'Is that so.'

'You forget brother, that kings have the power of life and death over their subjects.'

Oswiu laughed, 'Come, share what you know over a jug of ale, my King of Bernicia, I am your most humble subject.'

When Oswald saw King Cynegils next, he took Oswald aside clearly wishing to talk with him in private. Oswald prepared himself for the offer of his daughter in marriage, but nothing could have been further from the subject of an earthly marriage.

King Cynegils asked him if he would honour him by standing as his godfather at his baptism. Oswald was quite speechless at first, eventually saying to a nervously waiting King Cynegils that it would be an honour to stand with him.

Oswald knew that this would be all that Bishop Birinus could have hoped and prayed for, the conversion of a King often

meant in practice, the conversion of a
kingdom.

Chapter 24

Warrior – King – Saint

Oswald was cautious about the integrity of King Cynegils' conversion after his experience with Eanfrith who had merely used the church to his own ends and then when it suited him, reverted to his pagan past.

When he mentioned his doubts to Bishop Birinus, the Bishop asked who were they to judge the heart of another man.

At the very least, the Bishop was now able to preach the gospel freely and that was something of a miracle in itself.

On the day of the baptism, the weather was kind to them, and the sun shone for this new child of God, who this day would enter into the hope of eternity through this outward confession of a spiritual reality. This earthly king would now take on a new heavenly robe of righteousness.

Oswald prayed with King Cynegils, as his role of godfather dictated and assured the King that he would continue to support him in prayer, in the years to come. Whatever was the truth of this moment, Oswald had to admit that King Cynegils' confession of faith seemed sincere.

Dressed in a short-sleeved white robe King Cynegils was led into the river. Oswald smiled as he saw fish scatter before him, he remembered the fish scattering before the boat when he first went to Iona. King Cynegils knelt, holding his crown before him, clearly placing under God his kingship as well as his humanness.

Oswald stood on the riverbank holding towels. The Bishop scooped up water in a silver dish and poured it over King Cynegils' head, saying, 'I baptise you, Cynegils of the West Saxons, in the name of the Father, Son, and Holy Ghost.'

As the King walked out of the river towards Oswald, he nodded towards his assembled household who one by one followed his lead and were baptised. During the day the whole of the King's family and household were baptised into the Christian faith, including Princess Cyneburh.

At the feasting that night, Oswald decided to ask the Princess if she would return to Bernicia with him as his wife and Queen.

On asking her, her immediate reaction was to laugh. Over the weeks Oswald had been with the West Saxons, they had become easy friends, but this was a surprise. Her first thought was that he was teasing her, in the light of what she'd told him of her father's hopes. Oswald's disappointed face quickly dispelled that thought.

'Lord, forgive me for my cruelty, you are *truly* serious, aren't you?' Now she was solemn too and stared into his eyes. 'If I was to choose a husband he would be in your image, my dearest Oswald and Lord. If it is truly your wish then it is mine also.'

'Then it is decided,' and he embraced her, 'Princess, I cannot tell you how happy you have made me. I must talk with your father.'

This was all that King Cynegils had hoped for and he duly thanked the Christ God.

Oswald would return to Bernicia with his new Queen and an ally secured in the south.

As Oswald's entourage travelled slowly north, they visited town after town and village after village. Their subjects fell down before them, offering flowers and gifts and begging that he might pray for their sick.

These were good days and both Cyneburh and Oswald prayed each morning and night giving thanks to God, they could be in no doubt that their subjects saw him as a saintly person.

The first sight of Bebbanburg was all that Oswald said it was, it was more beautiful than Cyneburh had ever imagined it could be, set as it was in the rolling landscape of Bernicia, which sloped and meandered lazily down to the coast with its sandy beaches and blue sea. The view was simply stunning.

'Oswald, it is magnificent, I know that I will be happy here.'

All that Cyneburh said pleased Oswald for he loved his home.

They rode up the hill to the fortress and into the yard, standing there to greet them was none other than his old friends Abbot Ségéne and Brother Aidan from Iona. Oswald leapt from his horse and excitedly embraced them both, he didn't know where to start so much had happened since he'd last seen them.

'One moment,' he reached up to Cyneburh and lowered her to the ground. 'This, my friends, is my new Queen, Cyneburh, a child of the Living God, from the West Saxons, daughter of the newly converted King Cynegils.'

The Abbot and Brother Aidan bowed respectfully.

'I am honoured to meet the two men of whom my husband speaks so highly.'

296

'We have all been friends for many years my Lady, I pray that we might be numbered amongst *your* friends.'

'Then your prayer is answered,' she said laughing.

'Come, we have much to speak of, I am delighted to see you here, when did you arrive? I never expected such honoured guests.'

'Five days past, Lord, but our time has not been wasted,' Aidan told him.

'See to it that we have mete and drink in the hall,' Oswald ordered a servant as he passed.

'This is much grander than I am used to Oswald,' commented Cyneburh as she walked, and looked at all before her.

Hrodulf quickly joined them in the hall and with him came Oswald's son Æthelwald who leapt into his father's arms. Hrodulf embraced Oswald and Oswald introduced him to Cyneburh, he bowed to his new Queen and the Abbot.

'How are you my fine boy, I have missed you. I want you to meet a very special person whom I love and know you will grow to love too. Now take your arms from around my neck and, as I know you can, bow respectfully to this lady who is now your new mother and Queen of Bernicia.'

Æthelwald did as he was bidden, but with reservation, clearly he was not sure what this meant. Oswald was distracted for a moment then lifted Æthelwald once more onto his lap and turned his attention to the Abbot and Aidan.

Oswald said that he never imagined that the Abbot would come in person and to bring his old friend Aidan was more than he could have possibly hoped.

Abbot Ségéne told Oswald that Aidan was now a Bishop and that he'd been working in Hibernia. He had left that work to bring the gospel to Bernicia.

'Have you been to Lindis Feorna yet?'

'Indeed we have.'

'What did you think, Bishop Aidan?'

'We think it ideal, the perfect location to set up a community and we will reach out from there to the people of Bernicia.'

'We will need help and funds for the work,' added Abbot Ségéne.

'Fear not, you shall have all that you require. For this work of God is dearest to my heart.'

298

That night Oswald was so utterly overwhelmed by the joy he felt, he was unable to sleep. He walked and talked, sat, lay next to Cyneburh, then rose and walked some more, all the while she lay in their bed wrapped in his joy, how she loved this man.

Then he paused and lifted his finger to his nose as if struck by a sudden thought, and went to a small chest, opened it and withdrew something from it.

'I have something very special for you, it belonged to my mother, she never wore it, she once told me when I was young, younger than Æthelwald is now, that it had actually belonged to her sister. She said that the man she loved had given it to her. That meant nothing to me at the time, but it does now, I understand completely what she was saying and the significance of it.'

Oswald came to Cyneburh with his hands cupped together. Slowly he opened them like a clam revealing it's pearl, but when Oswald's hands opened inside was the largest most beautiful emerald she had ever seen on a gold chain.

She gasped, pressing her hand to her mouth. '*Oswald*, I have never seen anything like it in my life, it is beyond beauty.'

'Let me fasten it around your neck, where it belongs.'

299

'Where did it come from?'

'In truth, I know not. My mother, Queen Acha never wore it as far as I can recall, she showed it to me only the one time, when she told me it belonged to her sister. My mother, Queen Acha died on the island of Coll off the west coast of Alba, when I was living on Iona with the monks. Her belongings were packed and stored at Dunadd and I never opened them until they were brought here and that's when I found this and I remembered what she had once said to me.'

'I am so honoured, that you should give this to me.'

'It is more precious to me Cyneburh than you could ever imagine, as you are. It was given by a Lord Wulfstan to the Lady Aefre and they mean everything to me.'

'Who were they?'

'I will tell you the tale sometime, but not today.'

These were the happy years; Bernicia became a thriving kingdom with stability and wealth. Oswald's goodness and generosity as a King and ruler spread to all corners of Briton.

The work on Lindis Feorna was all Aidan and he had hoped for, they had been joined by more monks from Iona, all able and familiar with the work. Aidan's gentle self-effacing manner had suited the Bernician personality perfectly and they were growing to love the man.

Oswald was sorry that Cyneburh was not allowed on the island, they followed the same rules as the community on Iona, but Oswald told her in detail every stage of the work. He even made sketches for her so that she would have a better understanding.

One Easter feast at Bebbanburg where he'd invited Bishop Aidan to dine with him, a servant came to Oswald and told him there were beggars at the door asking for food. Oswald not only told him to feed them, but that the silver platter before him should be broken up and given to them.

'How can any man dine on such when there are men starving?'

Aidan had been so touched by Oswald's demonstration of kindness, that he had grasped his hand and prayed that it would never know corruption.

Oswald lifted his eyes from the letter he was reading and looked to Cyneburh who was busy with some needlework, by the window, 'I have had some disturbing correspondence from your father, Cyneburh, it appears that King Penda of Mercia is making war on the West Saxons, and I am sworn to help your people as their Overlord. I must raise an army and go south to give support as I have promised, and as soon as I can.'

'When, will that be, Lord?'

'It will need to be done as quickly as I can, otherwise it might be too late. Who knows how long I will be gone, but I must go as soon as I am able.'

The last few days had been hectic, but all was ready now. Oswald strode to his horse with the appearance of more confidence than he felt. He had rarely been separated from Cyneburh since they'd first met, which made this parting all the more difficult. She clung to his arm as he walked, and

Æthelwald who was now eighteen walked alongside them. Oswald was fully dressed for war, when he reached his horse, he paused with his hand on the saddle then turned to Æthelwald withdrew the Ulfberht from its frog and passed it to him.

'I will leave this precious thing in your safe keeping, Son, it means too much to me to risk it being stolen on my travels.'

'But Father...'

'Hush, I have other swords, but this one belonged to your grandfather, your mother here will tell you all, when she has a mind to. She knows all the history of this sword and its owner.'

Oswald wrapped Cyneburh in his arms, and she stared into his eyes, without thought, she reached up and tenderly slipped her finger through the centre of a grey curl on the side of his head as if noticing for the first time how the years had past. She drew it out between her finger and thumb – then she slowly released it, and wiped a tear from her cheek.

He lowered his head and tenderly pressed his lips to hers. When he tried to turn, she clung to him and refused to let him go...

'I can't do this Oswald, the pain is more than I can bear,' she whispered into his ear.

'My dearest Cyneburh, you are the Queen of Bernicia and you will be strong for

Bernicia.' He kissed her once more, smiled weakly, and gave her to Æthelwald to hold, 'Take care of your mother, my Son; I leave all in your hands. God bless and keep you both.'

'And you my dearest most precious husband.'

Oswald wearily mounted his waiting horse, leaned forward and patted its neck, nodded to his wife and son and he rode out of the gates, down the bank to the beach where his army eagerly awaited him.

Once he was with them, they moved off along the sand, southward, just as he had done so many times before. As the fort was about to disappear behind the sand dunes and out of his sight, he stopped and turned, while his army, rode passed him.

Finally, he was alone and he looked back towards the great fort of Bebbanburg. A gust of wind blew the silk scarf Cyneburh had tied to his arm and it fluttered before his eyes, and from it he caught the fragrance of her nearness. He knew his beloved wife Cyneburh, and his son Æthelwald would yet be watching, though he could no longer see them.

It was strange – thought Oswald, as he looked back to the fortress, silhouetted, as it was against the grey streaked Bernician sky. This view before him seemed to

304

symbolise and contain, most of his life, if any single view could, that is.

Strange... *strange* the things you remember, he thought. He thought of the people he'd known and loved, none more than Cedric, and his beloved Helen. The places, the moments in time burned into his heart forever, whilst others just fade into the mist. He'd always known he'd lived a life different from other men. He reflected on when he was a boy, and saw no path before him. He'd simply taken one step then another, ever rushing to a place he knew not where, and now he looked back and saw that each step he'd taken was a choice, to go left, or go right, to go forward or even not go at all. He could see so clearly now that every day one had choices to make, between right and wrong, love and hate, to forgive or not to forgive. Sometimes even between life and death and the sum of those choices, was the measure of a life lived.

He lowered his head; he could choose even now to ride back into the arms of his wife and son. Man's right to choose was God's costly gift to His children, which had ultimately cost Him His life.

Oswald knew that his mother and father had made choices, and each choice had played its part in *this* moment. He stared for a little while longer, searing the image into his mind, until the tears in his eyes made the edges of the skyline blurred. Then, with a heavy heart, he made the choice to honour his word – against the choice presented by his heart; slowly he turned his pony, and rode off...

Love is more than the time spent between hello and goodbye.

Author's Notes

Key:

[1] **Elne:** Saxon measurement 1 elne or ulna equals three feet/914.4mm (later yard)

[2] **Ad Gefrin:** So called by Bede, "Now known as Yeavering" is a twin-peaked hill near the river Glen in Northumbria, England, to the west of the village of Woller, and forming part of the Cheviot Hills. The hill, 361 metres above sea level, is encircled by the wall of a late-prehistoric "Hillfort", a tribal centre of the Votadini called in Brythonic and Old Welsh Din Gefron, from which the name stems from the Old English Geafringa.
  The hill fort encloses an area of approximately 12 acres. It was enclosed by a stonewall, which was upwards of 10 ft (3.0 m) thick, having four entrances into it. One of which is defended by a guardhouse. Within this area is an inner fort, excavated out of the rock, of an oval form, measuring 13 ft (4.0 m) across at the widest part. On the sides of the hill, and in a high valley

between the Bell and the next hill, called Whitelaw, there are many remains of stone huts rudely flagged. Some of them are in groups surrounded by rampiers (ramparts), and others isolated. Barrows, too, are numerous here. In the Annals of Cambriae, nearby River Glein is recorded as the site of the first of King Arthur's legendary twelve battles.

[3] Din Guyaroi: In 547 A.D. the ancient British coastal stronghold of Din Guyaroi (Bamburgh) on the North East coast was seized by the Angle chief called Ida the Flamebearer, who probably already had a foothold in the Tyne, Wear and Tees region. The name of this emerging kingdom, Bernicia, was probably an adaptation of an existing Celtic name and would come to be synonymous with the North Eastern region in the centuries to come. The rivers Tyne and Wear probably lay at the centre of this kingdom, which included most of present Northumberland and extended southwards to the Humber. Ida had conquered huge areas of land in the North East by 550 and was now undisputedly the most powerful leader in the northern Angle Land (later England). In 593, Aethelfrith, the grandson of Ida the Flamebearer, became the new King of Bernicia.

[4] Bebbanburg: It is clear that the name Bebbanburg was acceptable to the Æthelfrithings, in that it stayed attached to their main royal fortress and still does.

Aethelfrith and his sons are the ones who made Bernicia into a kingdom. Prior to Aethelfrith, Bernicia was little more than a Saxon stronghold, surrounded by Britons. It makes sense that Bebba was the queen of Aethelfrith and critically, I believe, for the name to have stuck on the fortress her son must have been a long and foundational king. Now, we know that Oswald's mother was Acha of Deira, so it can't be him. This really leaves us with King Oswiu, who reigned for 28 years. Oswiu is an ideal candidate for a son of Bebba who fixed her name to the fortress permanently.

[5] Leodwalding: were an Anglo Saxon aristocratic clan in Northumbria who claimed descent from King Ida of Bernicia. They played a prominent role in eighth century Northumbrian politics, providing several kings and prelates.

[6] Atheling: Old English for prince or lord.

[7] Abhainn Dubh: River Forth in Scotland.

[8] Abbot, Ségéne: Was a kinsman of Clom Cille (*Saint Columba*) He is credited with playing an active role amongst the Irish churches. It is tempting then to see Ségéne as the motivating force behind the Bernician conversions since he and Oswald enjoyed a close friendship, he had known Oswald while Abbot Fergno was head of the Iona community. It was through Ségéne that Oswald learned to speak fluent Irish.

[9] Lindisfarne: Today, often referred to as Holy Island, called by the Britons Metcaud.

[10] Dunadd: Originally occupied in the Iron Age, the site later became a seat of the kings of Dal Riata. It is known for its unique stone carvings below the upper enclosure, including a footprint and basin thought to have formed part of Dal Riata's coronation ritual. It is near Kilmartin in Argyll and Bute, Scotland On the west coast near Crinin Canal. Dunadd is one of the most significant archaeological sites in Scotland, and one of the most important early medieval sites in Britain. The site was excavated in 1980-81 by Dr Alan Lane of the Department of Archaeology, University of Cardiff.)

[11] Welsh: 607 A.D. And her Æþelfried lædde ferde to Legaceastre & þær ofsloh unrim Wealana. & swa wearþ gefylld Augustinus witegunge þe he cwæð, "gif Wealas nellaþ sibbe wið us, hie sculon æt Seaxena handa forweorþan."

(Translated) 607 A.D. And this year Ethelfrith (Æthelfrith) led a troop to Chester and there murdered a huge number of Welsh people and thus was fulfilled Augustine's prophecy when he said, "if the Welsh don't wish peace with us, they shall perish at the hands of the Saxons".

[12] Poet: Replaced Old English **scop** (which survives in scoff). The name was used for all sorts of writers, and composers of works of literature.

[13] Eostre: (*Ostara, Easter, Idhunn*): is thought by some to be the spring maiden. She is compared to Idunna, the goddess of vitality and health and is said to keep the apples that furnish the gods with eternal life. As the goddess of natural beauty and life just beginning, she is seen as ever jubilant and frolicking. The only account of her existence is made by Bede in the

Reckoning of Time, and the modern holiday of Easter is named for her. It is still debated whether-or-not Bede is correct in his conclusion that she is a goddess worshiped by the Anglo-Saxons.

[14] Celtic knots: are complete loops without any beginning or end; this unending style is called pure knots. The knots vary from simple to complicated ones. The use of only one thread highlights the Celts' belief in the interconnectedness of life and eternity.

[15] A Curragh: was an Irish boat, which could carry at least twelve people. It was made of oak laths and tarred canvas. The boats were very flexible and need special oars with very thin blades to prevent too much stress/torque on the side of the boat frame.

[16] **Thwart:** a board that spans the boat and serves the dual purpose of distributing the load on the structure by tying the sides together, and at the same time, creating place for crew and passengers to sit. (See above)

[17] **Muile:** The island of Mull off the western coast of Scotland.

[18] **An Crìonan:** Crinin a village on the west coast of Scotland. The Crinin Canal is a waterway with one of its outlets at Crinan, linking Loch Fyne with Loch Crinan.

[19] **Sluagad Fiachnae meic Báetáin:** No historical sources for Fiachnae's life now remain, excepting a few bald entries in the Irish Annals. A number of later traditions and a lost poem called Sluagad Fiachnae meic Báetáin co Dún nGuaire i Saxanaib, The hosting of Fiachnae mac Báetáin to *Dún Guaire* (**Bamburgh** in Northumbria England) in the kingdom of the Saxons) suggest that he was a significant figure in his time. He campaigned against King Edwin of Northumbria and perhaps also his predecessor King Æthelfrith. He may have

captured Bamburgh, - or only besieged it - circa 623.

[20] Sutton Hoo Helmet: In 1939, with World War II about to begin, archaeologists in Britain were excited by a discovery from 1,300 years ago.

Inside a grassy mound at Sutton Hoo, in Suffolk, they unearthed the remains of an Anglo-Saxon ship, possibly the tomb of a 7th-century nobleman, thought to be King Rædwald.

The wooden ship had rotted away, but its outline, and some of the treasures buried with it remained. Among the gold, silver and iron was a sword, a shield and this warrior's helmet, probably the most famous of all Anglo-Saxon museum treasures.

[21] Dál Riata (also Dalriada or Dalriata) was a Gaelic over-kingdom that included parts of western Scotland and northeastern Ireland, on each side of the North Channel, which connects the Irish Sea to the Atlantic Ocean. In the late 6th – early 7th centuries it encompassed roughly, what is now Argyll in Scotland and County Antrim in the Irish province of Ulster.

[22] Ulfberht:

Ulfberht is a name given to unique Viking swords. The high-quality steel they used remained unparalleled until the Industrial Revolution. 171 such swords have been found so far, but only a few of these have been proven authentic Ulfberht swords. The earliest Ulfberhts date from circa 850.

Little information is available about the fabrication of the Ulfberht sword. However, modern tests reveal that genuine Ulfberht swords were forged from crucible steel, which is the purest form of steel. While most medieval weapons were made of soft iron with little carbon, an Ulfberht had a much higher level of carbon and less slag. This made the weapon stronger, more flexible, and therefore less likely to break and easier to remove from enemy shields. The technology was likely acquired by Vikings who travelled to Central Asia. Using speculative techniques, modern-day blacksmith Richard Furrer made a replica of an Ulfberht. He can be seen making it on "You Tube".

The Ulfberht gave those who wielded it, a significant advantage, and was probably carried only by elite warriors and chieftains, a high status symbol of great expense and prestige. Porsche, GUCCI, ROLEX, or Aston Martin would make a similar statement today.

Although of similar size and shape to a common Viking sword, the Ulfberht was far more durable, and penetrated armour more easily. The characteristic identifying mark is the metallic inlay "+VLFBERH+T" on the flat of the blade close to the hilt (the variation "+VLFBERHT+" was inlaid in swords made from lower-quality steel, much in the same way a the Nike, or Rolex brand may be copied in today's market place). The sword's primary purpose was to break through an enemy's shield and chain mail armour. An Ulfberht's blade was very flexible compared to other weapons of the time and would not break or be held fast as easily when slicing into wood, striking steel, or even flesh, thus giving the swordsman opportunity to move on quickly after cutting down a foe.

"Ulfberht" is possibly a Frankish word whose meaning is unknown. The inscription "+(U)VLFBERH+T" used Latin letters.

The most common hypotheses are: that it was the name of a sword smith who passed his craft on to apprentices or family members, or that it was the name of a group of craftsmen. The word is possibly a compound of the elements *Ulfr* "Wolf" (old Norse) and *beraht,* "Light, bright, shining" (old high German, old Saxon).

In May 2008, at Christie's, £9350 was paid for an original Ulfberht sword in excavated condition, circa 950 AD.

[23] Burials: The remains of 110 individuals have been found in the sand dunes near Bamburgh Castle in Northumbria. In 2016, they were laid to rest in St Aidan's Church in Bamburgh more than 1300 years after they died. By taking DNA from their teeth at least one of the skeletons, can be identified as having lived on Iona, possibly a monk.

We also know, that one of them was a warrior named Cedric and a prayer was answered. It must be true it's in the story.

[24] The Lord's Prayer: "Old English" is a version of English spoken from approximately AD 450 to about 1100, and was in use in much of England and southeast Scotland. It also known as "Anglo-Saxon", and is a combination of the Germanic based languages of Old Norse and Old Frisian, and Latin.

(Note: the old English "þ" is pronounced "th")

Fæder ure þu þe eart on heofonum;
Si þin nama gehalgod
to becume þin rice
gewurþe ðin willa
on eorðan swa swa on heofonum.
urne gedæghwamlican hlaf syle us todæg
and forgyf us ure gyltas
swa swa we forgyfað urum gyltendum
and ne gelæd þu us on costnunge
ac alys us of yfele soþlice.

[25] Whiteblade: Oswald was known as Oswald **(Lamnguin)** Whiteblade the name is Irish and must have been given to him during his exile amongst the Scots between the age of twenty and thirty, when he returned to Northumbria.

[26] Muine Mór: Moneymore in Ireland (from Irish: meaning "Large thicket or large hill") is a village in County Londonderry, Northern Ireland. It is situated within Mid-

Ulster District. It is an example of a plantation village in Mid-Ulster.

[27] Fid Eóin: the exact location of the battle is unknown.

In the Chronicon Scotorum (Author: unknown)

Anal CS629
The battle of Fid Eoin in which Mael Caích son of Scannal, i.e. the king of the Cruithin was victor. The Dál Riata fell, and Díucaill son of Eochu king of the Cruithin people fell, and Aedhan's descendants, i.e. Rigullan son of Conaing and Faelbhe son of Eochaid and Oric son of Albirit, heir designate of Saxan, with a great slaughter of their followers.

[28] Saint Æbbe: Abb or Ebba is sometimes known as Æbbe the Elder to avoid confusion with a later Saint Æbbe. She lived from 615 to 25 August 683.
Æbbe was born a princess, the daughter of King Aethelfrith of Bernicia and his wife Acha of Deira. Aethelfrith had married Acha in 604 after invading Deira, and becoming the first King of a unified Northumbria. In 616, the deposed King Edwin of Deira returned from exile and defeated Aethelfrith to become the second

King of Northumbria. Aethelfrith's children, including Æbbe, were sent to safety in the court of King Domnall Brecc of Dalriada. While in exile they were converted to Christianity by the followers of Saint Columba.

[29] **Cear Luel**: modern day Carlisle in the North of England.

[30] **Hefenfelth:** Heavenfield in where Oswald camped in Northumbria England.

[31] **Colm Cille:** Saint Columba of Iona.

[32] **Hagustaldesham:** Hexham in Oswald's Northumbria.

[33] **Divelis:** Is now called Devils Water, near Hexham in Northumbria.

[34] **Caer Urfa:** South Shields is a coastal town at the mouth of the River Tyne at the eastern end of the Roman Wall. It had been a supply depot for the wall when it was a border defence of the Romans.

[35] **Winterfilleð:** The Anglo-Saxon lunar month corresponding to **October** was *Winterfilleð*, according to the Venerable Bede.

[36] Bēamford: They clashed at the Battle of "Win & Lose Hill" Modern day Bamford in the Derbyshire peak district.

Oswald's Time line

- 603: King Ælla of Deira must have died and **Æthelfrith became king** and drove out Edwin King Ælla's.
- 605: Born: 605ish.
- 605: Battle of Degsastan... *(Wulfstan & Aefre Die)*
- 606: In 611 Æthelfrith defeats **Ælla** (Æthelfrith must have killed Ælla) King the now King of Deira and marries Acha, Edwin's sister.
- 610: Æthelfrith marries Bebba, possibly a Pictish princess.
- 611: Oswiu is born to Bebba.
- 612: Æbbe Born to Bebba.
- 616: Æthelfrith killed at the battle of the river Idle by Edwin & King Rædwald of East Anglia.

The Story begins in 616...

(Age) Date

- (11) **616**: Oswald and his family escaped to King Eochaid Buide, who Colm Cille had prophesied to his father would be king at the Dalriadan court. (Oswald would be 11ish)

Æthelfrith eldest son's mother (Born around 590ish) was probably Pictish and may well have been related to King Eochaid Buide one of two possible reasons why they went to Æthelfrith's enemy for shelter. The other reason is that Queen Bebba who married Æthelfrith may well also have been related to King Eochaid Buide.

- (12) **617**: Oswald went to Iona to study, Acha went to live on Coll. Bebba, may well have stayed at Dunadd the court of King Eochaid Buide.
- (12) **617** The Abbot of Iona is now Fergno Brit, probably a Briton. (Died in 623)
- (15) **620**: Eanfrith marries a Pictish princess, Edlin (Invented name) possibly King Eochaid Buide's daughter.

- (17) **622**: Eanfrith has a son, Talorcan, who becomes King of the Picts.

While no historical sources for Fiachnae's life now remain, excepting a few bald entries in the "Irish Annals", a number of later traditions and a lost poem called Sluagad Fiachnae meic Báetáin co Dún nGuaire i Saxanaib (The hosting of Fiachnae mac Baetain to Dun Guaire (Bamburgh) in the kingdom of the Saxons) suggest that he was a significant figure in his time, campaigning against King Edwin of Bernicia and perhaps also against Edwin's predecessor King Æthelfrith. He may have captured Bamburgh - or only besieged it - circa 623.

- (17) **622**: Oswald offers his sister Æbbe in marriage to Prince Domnall Brecc (King Eochaid Buide's son, nicknamed "Freckled Donald") of Dalriada, but she refuses and enters the Church.
- (18) **623**: 617The Abbot of Iona, Fergno Brit, died.
- (18) **623**: Abbot, Ségéne replaced Fergno Brit and was one of the longest serving Abbots of Iona. He served until 652. (29 years)

- **(20) 624: In my story, Oswald marries Princess Helen.**

- (23) 628: King Eochaid Buide died now 45. *(Born 583 he would have been 33 when he met Oswald)*
- (23) 628: Oswald fought with the new King Conadd Cerr in Ireland against Maelcaich, at the battle of Fid Eóin. King Conadd Cerr was killed in the battle and was succeed by his brother, Prince Domnall Brecc.

- **(24) 629: Helen Dies in child berth.**

See note: Age (31) in 636.
In my story Oswald's son Æthelwald born, in 629 this would make him 19 when he became king which has been suggested by some scholars.

- (28) **633**: King Edwin killed by Cadwallon of Gwynedd & Penda of Mercia when they invaded Northumbria.
- (28) **633**: Æthelfrith's eldest son Eanfrith returns to claim his throne. As soon as he becomes king, he renounces his Christian faith and

returns to his pagan ways. He befriends Cadwalla or Cadwallon, *(As with all the names of this time there are many differing spellings)* and is tricked, by going to Cadwallon with only 12 men to negotiate peace and is murdered.

- (29) **634**: Oswald's raven comes on the scene.
- (29) **634**: Oswald becomes King. There is a tradition that Oswald became king on what is now known as the Lawe Top at South Shields, in the olden days it was known as Oswald's Hill.
- (29) **634**: Oswald takes an army to defeat Cadwallon and meets him at Heavenfield (Hefenfelth). The Welsh army advance north from York. Oswald positions his smaller army beside the Roman wall about four miles north of Hexham. He has a vision in his tent of Saint Columba who assures him of victory. Oswald erects a cross. His army faces east with Brady's crag on one side and the wall on the other which creates a narrow front for Cadwallon's army.
- (30) **635**: Oswald marries Cyneburh, *(Only once her name appears and that is as Kyneburga in Reginald of*

Durham's 12ᵗʰ century writing) the daughter of King Cynegils Wessex in order to expand his territory and Christianity. Oswald stands as godfather to King Cynegils. I suspect Oswald's wife's name would have been spelt with a "C" rather than a "K" thus my different spelling. In 1938 Henry Bosley Woolf showed that Old English female names have a high probability of *alliteration* with their father's name, and that is what I have assumed. It is not difficult to see the connection to the 12th century spelling.

- (31) **636**: Oswald and Cyneburh have a son *Æthelwald*. Æthelwald begins to rule in 651, which means he would only have been 15 years old. *It is thought to be highly unlikely that in this period of history, when a strong leader was considered to be essential, that a boy of 15 would be elected to be king. This has lead some to wonder if he was the son from a relationship whilst Oswald was in exile at the Dalriadan court. It is known that Oswald's brother Oswiu had at least two children when they lived in exile.*

- (32) **637**: Oswald sent for Aidan, he comes and blesses Oswald's arm, which is said to be then incorruptible.
- (33) **638**: Oswald conquers Edinburgh and his brother Oswiu marries Princess Rhiainfelt, the last princess of North Rheged
- (38) **642**: Oswald now 37/38, is killed at Masterfield now Oswestry in Shropshire...

St. Oswald subdued the kingdom of the Mercians and drove the pagan King Penda into exile in Wales. However, in 642 Penda gathered a large heathen army and, allying himself with the Welsh ruler of the mid-Severn valley Cynddylan, he unexpectedly attacked Oswald near Oswestry. "But the man of God," writes Reginald of Durham, "hitherto renowned for his honour as a soldier, refused to consider flight, in case he should seem a man unskilled in the conduct of battle. He considered it dishonourable to be found vanquished and disgraced at the end, when hitherto he had appeared to all to be a vigorous and victorious warrior. And so he summoned a small force of soldiers and proceeded to commit himself to Christ, gladly choosing to die for the honour of the Lord and the faith of the Cross, and for the salvation and freedom of his Christian people... He therefore advanced to battle with great confidence, seeing that he was summoned by the Lord's mercy to a martyr's crown. Penda had gathered a large force of the heathen, and suddenly advanced to the field of battle, where he slaughtered a great number of the Christian people together with their holy and most Christian king. "Bede records that when the saint "saw that he was surrounded by enemy forces and about to be slain, he prayed for the souls of his army; and this is the origin of the proverb. 'God have mercy on their souls,' said Oswald falling to the ground.

Penda took the saint's head and hands and fixed them on stakes for a whole year, to be an object of derision and scorn. His head was later retrieved by his brother Oswiu, and was placed in St. Cuthbert's coffin, where it still remains. His right hand - the one St. Aidan had blessed - was placed in a silver casket at Bamburgh, where it remained completely incorrupt until at least the twelfth century, as both Abbot Aelfric and Simeon of Durham attest. At the place where he died - praying, with arms outstretched, for the souls of his men - many miracles were wrought.

In the year 697 Queen Ostrythe of Mercia, who was the saint's niece, and was later murdered herself, decided with her husband King Ethelred to translate the relics of the saint to the monastery of Bardney in Lindsey (Lincolnshire). But the monks of that monastery, entertaining a grudge against Oswald because he had once been king over that region, refused to allow the relics through the monastery gates. So, they remained on a wagon covered by a tent throughout the night.

However, during the night a great column of light was seen stretching from the wagon up to heaven, which was visible throughout Lindsey. Chastened, the monks brought the holy relics inside the gates, washed them with reverence, and placed them in a specially constructed shrine in the church with a gold and purple banner over it. The water used in the washing was poured away in a corner; but the earth, which had received it was found to have the power of expelling demons.

Other books by this author:

Restoration (Book 1)

This is a saga; spread over two novels telling of impossible love, its path travelled, and the tension between relationships, honour, pride, privilege, resentment, hate, and forgiveness.

Acceptance (Book 2)

The series plots a family's journey through the period of history from 1900 to 1946 the fears, sadness, and uncertainties of two world wars with their lottery of life and death, the only constant is love and the product of love, hope.

Set in the North East of England.

The Man Who Lived In A Book

A murder mystery set in the Marshall Islands. You may well solve the murder but miss the mystery.

Detective Inspector Tyyamii has a great future, how would you like to be his assistant in the Marshall Islands?

Swallows Leave In Autumn

Set in the North East of England with its miles of beautiful golden beaches, blue sea and historic castles, the home of international author, Sebastian Swan.

Tom Jackson decides to step out of the "Rat race" and rent a cottage in a quiet fishing village on the north east coast of Northumbria. He'd recently resigned from his job as a schoolteacher. Work he had grown to hate.

Tom had a first-class honours degree in fine art. His lecturers told him he was "Exceptional".

He was now going to try to make a living as an artist, and see if "Exceptional" would sell enough paintings to put bread on his table.

One summer's evening Tom was sitting on a bench, relaxing mindlessly in the sun watching the swallows swoop back and forth, as they sliced through the sunlight before him. Glancing along the beach his eye caught sight of a young woman in the distance. She drew nearer and nearer, walked up the path to where he was seated, sat down beside him and smiled. This was to be the moment his life changed forever.

Tom never imagined what he would have to face. They came from different worlds, which inevitably brought conflict to their relationship. They were to discover the sharp reality that "True love" can be a very painful path to tread.

Sebastian Swan invites you to walk, laugh, and cry with them.
International Author Sebastian Swan's latest page-turner.

The Colour of Envy (Ulfberht Book 4)

Set in the Reign of Henry II.

On hearing of the fortunes to be made at the tournais in France, a young knight, Richard Maillorie, sees a way to restore his family's fortune and becomes a friend of the great William Marshal. On his return from France, he meets the beautiful Julianne and a complicated journey of love and jealousy begins.

Driven by Honour (Ulfberht Book 5)

A sequel to "The Colour of Envy" a chance to follow the lives through the history of three kings culminating in the reign of King John accredited with the title of the most evil King in history.

The Price of Honour (Ulfberht Book 1)

The setting is Bernicia, circa (Northumbria) 600 AD

Wulfstan, a young warrior known throughout the north for his bravery and honour, is asked to seek a bride for his King, Æthelfrith. She is the beautiful Princess Aefre, the daughter of King Ælla of Deira.
The gods pour on them their magic potion and their future is sealed.
Are they wicked, or merely playthings of the gods, and to be pitied?

You decide.

The Carnelian Ring

SAS Captain Robert Mallory and his Maggie, invite some old friends, Keith and Irene, round for lunch. During the meal, the conversation soon focuses on a ring Robert found that morning in the garden. Keith is intrigued, but Robert tells him he must not touch it for fear of being injured, for he suspects that the ring holds within it the strange power of Synchronicity.

However, Robert does not heed his own advice.

Resulting in him being faced with an impossible choice.

Plato said, "time is an imperfect reflection, it is merely the moving image of eternity".

If the reader has any comments about the book, the author would be pleased to hear from you.

sebastian.dave.swan@gmail.com

17507381R00190

Printed in Great Britain
by Amazon